Gamers' Challenge

George Ivanoff is an author and stay-at-home dad residing in Melbourne, Australia. He has written over 50 books for children and teenagers. His teen science fiction novel, *Gamers' Quest*, won a 2010 Chronos Award for speculative fiction. He has books on both the Victorian Premier's and the NSW Premier's Reading Challenge booklists. George eats too much chocolate and drinks too much coffee. He has one wife and two children. Check out George's website at: www.georgeivanoff.com.au

The Official Gamers' Quest website for stories, music and videos is at: http://www.gamersquestbook.com

For my good friend, H. Gibbens, and my favourite brother-in-law, Marc Valko. Many thanks for the awesome visuals and music

GAMERS' CHALLENGE

George Ivanoff

First published by Ford Street Publishing, an imprint of
Hybrid Publishers, PO Box 52, Ormond VIC 3204

Melbourne Victoria Australia

© George Ivanoff 2011
2 4 6 8 10 9 7 5 3 1

This publication is copyright. Apart from any use
as permitted under the Copyright Act 1968, no part
may be reproduced by any process without prior written
permission from the publisher. Requests and enquiries
concerning reproduction should be addressed to
Ford Street Publishing Pty Ltd
2 Ford Street, Clifton Hill VIC 3068.
Ford Street website: www.fordstreetpublishing.com

First published 2011

National Library of Australia Cataloguing-in-Publication entry:
Author: Ivanoff, George 1968–
Title: Gamers' Challenge / George Ivanoff
ISBN: 9781921665516 (pbk.)
Target audience: For secondary school age
Dewey Number: A823.3

Cover art: © Les Petersen
Cover design: © Grant Gittus Graphics
In-house editor: Beau Hillier

Printed in China by Tingleman Pty Ltd

Contents

Prologue	1
1: Zyra	2
2: Tark	8
3: Explanations	14
4: The Outers	26
5: Familiar Faces	35
6: Tark and Zyra	41
7: Hope	45
8: Sanctuary	58
9: Jump	66
10: Legend of the Ultimate Gamer	70
11: Left Behind	77
12: Now What?	80

13: The Thing in the Cave	85
14: Brains!	89
15: IDD	94
16: No-man's-land	98
17: Testing	109
18: Pinball	115
19: Reload	122
20: Bobby	129
21: Ready to Devour	135
22: Bobby and the Fat Man	142
23: Preparations	145
24: Antibodies	148
25: The Ultimate Gamer	154
26: Battle in the Light Grid – Chimaera vs Knight	160
27: Charging Up	163
28: Battle in the Light Grid – Dragon vs Unicorn	167
29: Super-charged	170

30: Battle in the Light Grid –
    Static Man vs Fat Man   173

31: Plans   176

32: Battle in the Light Grid – Endgame 181

33: Overload   184

34: Goodbyes   189

Acknowledgements   193

Prologue

It all started with a kiss.
　Everything changed.
　Or was it that everything stayed the same . . . except them?

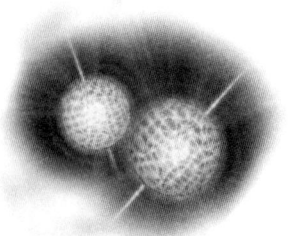

1: Zyra

Zyra took aim, almost saying a prayer to the Designers out of habit, and pulled the trigger. She watched the crossbow bolt slice through the air, pinning all her hopes on it as it made its way to its target. Could this bolt be different? Could the fact that it belonged to the monks from the Temple of Paths be the deciding factor?

But just like every other weapon Zyra had tried, the bolt did not do its job. It froze as it met its target. Pixel by pixel, it was deconstructed and absorbed into the grey, sizzling nothingness.

Zyra pulled the second trigger to fire the auxiliary bolt, more out of frustration than any real hope of it working. It too was taken apart and removed from the World.

'Blast!' Zyra tossed the useless crossbow to one side.

The writhing mass of static shot towards her. Zyra flung herself to the ground and rolled, her shoulder crunching painfully over the rubble, then sprang to her feet and ran. The vaguely spherical conglomeration of static streaked after her.

Zyra knew she couldn't outrun it – but she could stay ahead of it, at least for a little while. She'd had lots of practice recently, as each weapon she'd tested inevitably failed.

Sprinting along the cracked and crumbling roads of the City, her worn red leather coat flapping about her legs, she felt sweat prickling her brow. She skirted the ruins of a large building, almost losing her footing in the rubble, but managing to retain her balance. She didn't need to look behind to know that in the second it took to stop herself from falling, the inexplicable ball of static would have gained ground. One more misplaced step, the slightest mistake, and she'd be dead – deconstructed, pulled apart, molecule by molecule. She could feel her heart pounding in her chest, the fear rising up inside her, the sweat now dripping from her face.

Zyra rounded another corner in a spray of gravel and ran into the graveyard that backed onto the Temple of Paths. She had concealed another loaded crossbow in the shrubbery that grew amongst the multitude of dilapidated headstones, but saw little reason in using it now. She'd be dead before she could pick up the crossbow and even if she could fire it, it would have no effect. She had only one hope. Her eyes locked onto the vestry at the end of the graveyard, a ramshackle stone room tacked on to one side at the back of the Temple of Paths. The static was right behind her. The second it took to open the door would mean the end of her.

Lungs burning, heart pounding, Zyra vaulted a headstone and made for the little window beside the vestry door, the glass long ago shattered and never replaced. A good couple of strides before reaching the window, she leapt into the air. Arms outstretched, she dived through the glassless frame. Relief washed over her as she thudded onto the thin mattress.

Winded, she took a moment to catch her breath and pull the hair back from her eyes, and then rolled off the mattress, slowly getting to her feet. As she turned and looked at the window frame, she could see the static hovering outside. Zyra stepped over to the window and leant in close, until her face was centimetres from the basketball-sized conglomeration of simmering menace. She ran her fingers along the growing stubble that surrounded her red Mohawk.

'Can't gets me in 'ere.'

The static rolled and writhed and bubbled, like a starving animal separated from its prey. Questions floated through Zyra's mind. What were these things? How did they maintain their shape? After all, they had no real substance. They were just static, like what you would see on an un-tuned television set, or in that unreal place between game environments. And why were they after her?

Zyra stared into its fathomless depths, watching the grey nothingness. She felt like it would be so easy to just give in; to reach out a hand, touch it, and let it consume her.

Something formed, bared its fangs, and then the static – and whatever it was within its cold depths – was no longer there.

Zyra staggered backwards, tripping and landing hard on the stone floor, her bones jarring.

'Imagination,' she told herself, tugging at one of the studs that pierced her lower lip. 'Just imagination.'

She rose slowly, wincing with pain, and yawned. In addition to the homicidal static and her and Tark's inability to interact with the game, something else had changed. Ever since their rebellious, rule-breaking kiss, both Zyra and Tark seemed to have become more susceptible to aches and pains and fatigue. It used to be that, when injured, Zyra would bounce back quickly, all residual effects disappearing. But not anymore. Gone were the days when bruises never formed, falls were barely noticed and near-asphyxiation could be shaken off within minutes. Gone were the days when she only slept between adventures. She rubbed at her aching shoulder, stretched her jarred back and yawned again.

She and Tark had broken the Designers' rules. She knew that . . . and she accepted that there would be consequences. She could live with the aches and pains; she could deal with having to sleep regularly; she didn't especially care that they were no longer part of the game that continued to unfold around them. Even the pimples that had started to pop out on her face were endurable. But deadly static appearing out of nowhere and trying to kill her? That was another matter.

It wouldn't be so bad if the static was after Tark as well. But these random manifestations had singled her out. It wasn't that they didn't attack Tark when they came across him. They did. But it was her they wanted. Within minutes of leaving the Temple of Paths, at least one of the blasted things would be upon her. Tark, meanwhile, seemed to be able to roam around, so long as he was careful and she wasn't present. She hated that!

Not for the first time, Zyra wondered if they had made a mistake. Their lives had been a lot simpler when they had been playing the game. If they hadn't kissed, they would still be playing.

Zyra shook the thought from her mind and looked around the vestry. She supposed that she should feel grateful that she was safe in here, even though she didn't know why. It was little more than a small room added onto the back of the Temple. None of the monks ever seemed to use it. Apart from an old table and a pile of robes, it had been empty when she and Tark had found it. Now it contained a couple of old straw-stuffed mattresses, some worn blankets and a small stash of food. They had also accumulated a reasonable batch of weapons, poorly concealed under the robes. Every so often, Tark would go out and scavenge anything of use that he could find.

Zyra wandered over to the pile of robes and lifted them back. Guns, knives, throwing stars, a sword and some nunchucks. There had been two crossbows earlier on, before she had decided to try them out. She had thought they might work. After all, the Temple of Paths kept the static at bay. It was logical to assume that the weapons of the monks within might have some effect. But no.

A stray bit of hair flopped in front of her eyes and she swept it back roughly. She missed that her hair used to just stay in place, nice and spiky, instead of draping all over the place.

In the distance, Zyra could hear the monks chanting.

'Don't they eva stop?' Then she yelled, 'SHUDDUP!'

A strand of hair dropped down in front of her eyes again.

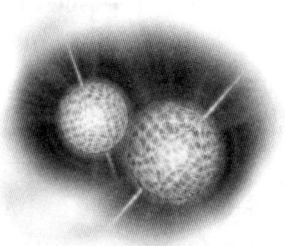

2: Tark

Tark leaned up against a tree and waited. Once upon a time he would have been wrapped in his magik cloak, perched upon a high branch, out of view. But now there was no need. He stood at the edge of the path, waiting for a travelling princeling, knowing that he would not be noticed and hoping to steal something of use.

He was dressed, as always, in ill-fitting, drab, brown leggings and a tunic, with high black boots that were still in reasonable condition. At least some things hadn't changed. He ran a hand through his black hair. Now that was something different. His hair had never grown before. It had always been little more than stubble. He closed his hand into a fist, catching the hair between his fingers. If it kept growing, he would have to start cutting it.

Tark's hand dropped and his head snapped to the right as he heard the rustling of leaves. His violet eyes stared into the undergrowth, looking for movement. Dense foliage grew right up to the edge of the path concealing what lay within the depths of the Forest. The perfect hiding place, thought Tark. Not that he needed a hiding place anymore. The sound of hooves along the path made him turn his attention to the other direction.

Rounding the bend, he could see a man on a horse. The rider was richly dressed and the stallion pranced.

'Show-off!' muttered Tark.

Following close behind was a mule, pulling a wagon. A pageboy rode on the mule's back, as it strained to haul its load. As they neared, Tark could see that the man's clothes, though rich, were quite old and slightly shabby. The pageboy's attire was also very worn and grubby. The cart contained only a few wooden chests (no doubt filled with what remained of the man's fortune), some clothing and a meagre selection of fruits and vegetables.

'Oh, great,' whispered Tark. 'Justs a no-longer-rich dude, wot somethin' rough happened ta.' Still, it would have to do. Beggars couldn't be choosers.

Tark waited and watched as the small entourage approached and passed. Falling in line behind the cart, Tark swiftly relieved it of several apples. Pocketing them, he reached for the nearest trunk, but found he couldn't grasp it. His hand was simply unable to make contact.

'Blast!' Tark hated the way that happened. The fact that no one seemed able to see him had certainly aided in the acquisition of supplies, but the fact that he was also unable to interact with so many things was a real hindrance. As far as he and Zyra could work out, it seemed that anything important to the game, was out of bounds to them.

Tark's mind was drawn back to the kiss that had changed everything for him. He absently brought a hand up to his chin and started picking at the pimple that had sprung up there. Had they done the right thing in defying the Designers? He wasn't sure. Life was certainly more difficult now. But he also felt as if an invisible weight had been lifted from his shoulders. He was free now. He could do what he wanted. He didn't have to continually steal money. He was no longer reliant on getting to. Designers Paradise to be happy. He didn't have to worry about the Designers' ridiculous rules. He was allowed to kiss Zyra whenever he wanted . . . if only she would let him.

His pimple oozed a little pus and began to bleed.

***

A man peered out through the leaves and watched Tark intently. He wore a dark hooded cloak and crouched in the undergrowth by the side of the path.

'At long last,' he murmured.

He scratched at his beard and continued to watch as Tark ate one of the stolen apples. Realising that the boy would soon be on his way, the hooded man decided that now was as good a time as any. Rising slowly to his feet, he adjusted his cloak and stepped out through the bushes onto the path.

Tark stared in his direction, eyes widening. Dropping his apple core, he produced two throwing stars from the pouch on his belt.

'Damn!' This was not the reaction the man had been hoping for.

***

'Behind you!' Tark shouted, even though he knew that there was no way that the hooded man could hear him. He was as unheard as he was unseen in the World since the kiss.

To Tark's amazement the man turned to look back, then threw himself to the ground, giving Tark a clear shot at the ball of static that had emerged from the trees. Tark threw the stars and quickly fished another two from his pouch.

The undulating sphere of static froze in the air as it picked apart and consumed the shaped metal. With the stars gone, it pulsed and roiled again, but did not advance, seemingly undecided as to who to attack first. Taking advantage of this hesitation, the hooded man sprang to his feet, unhooking the small crossbow that hung from his belt. The ball of static moved towards him.

'Distract it!' he yelled at Tark.

If there had been time to think, Tark would have been amazed that this mysterious stranger had not only seen him, but was now yelling at him. Given the circumstances, however, Tark's thoughts were otherwise occupied. He threw another two stars.

The static froze as the stars were deconstructed once again. Then it shifted its attention from the hooded man to Tark. As it bubbled and pulsated, Tark imagined that he could see images forming within its depths, before being swallowed by the sizzling nothingness. He couldn't make out what they were, but he had a sense of malice and hunger.

From the corner of his eye, Tark saw the hooded man load his crossbow, take aim, and fire. As the bolt shot through the air, the man was already reloading.

The first bolt stuck home. The ball of static sparked and crackled, its edges flaring and dissolving as its movement toward Tark ceased. The diminishing mass turned its attention away from Tark and back towards the hooded man. His crossbow was reloaded, aimed and ready to fire.

Tark saw that the bolt was tipped with static. It flew through the air and struck their attacker. The sphere burst apart, its insubstantial greyness flaring and dissipating in all directions, until there was nothing left.

Tark watched warily as the man returned the small but effective crossbow to his belt and approached him. His hood was still in place, concealing much of his face, but Tark glimpsed a grey beard.

'Thank you.' The man's voice was deep and a little gravely, but also vaguely familiar to Tark.

'Ya can sees me?' The enormity of the situation finally hit Tark.

'Obviously,' the man replied. 'I can see you. I can hear you. I can interact with you.' He offered his gloved hand to Tark.

'How?' snapped Tark, immediately suspicious, ignoring the outstretched hand.

'I'm not playing the Designers' game either,' he said simply. He held up his hand to stop Tark from asking further questions. 'We are still in danger. If one VI has been able to find us, then there's the distinct possibility of more.'

'VI?'

'The ball of static. It's a Viral Interface,' explained the man. 'Or, at least, that is what we call them. Now we should get out of here. Ideally, we need to get to Zyra before any more VIs show up. I assume you know where she is and can take me there?'

'How does ya know about Zyra?' Tark's voice rose. 'Wot is these viral things?' His hand slipped down to the pouch with the stars. 'And who the hell is ya?'

'We don't have time for this now. I'm a friend and I'm here to help you. But we need to get to Zyra.'

Tark did not move. His muscles were tense and rigid. He eyed the stranger, ready to fight if necessary.

'Please!' said the man. His hood shifted a little and Tark saw violet eyes staring out at him, pleadingly. 'I promise that I will explain everything once I am sure that Zyra is safe.'

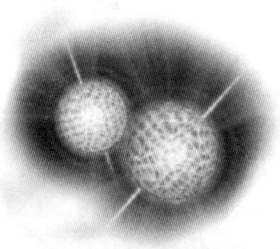

3: Explanations

The monks' chanting voices filled the Temple of Paths as they knelt on the flagstone floor. Every now and then, one of the monks would prostrate himself, heavy brown robes pooling on the floor around him, before returning to his knees and his chanting. The head monk, robed in red, knelt on a raised area at the end of the Temple, his cowled head just visible behind the altar. Brocaded drapes of bronze and purple hung on the wall behind him.

A row of television screens on sconces, each displaying the image of flickering candles, lined the two longer walls. More screens hung from the ceiling joists, displaying nothing but static. Between the joists of the vaulted ceiling and the sconced screens, four booths protruded from the wall like opera boxes, each with a Designers Paradise logo – the letters DP intertwined in a silver and gold swirl.

Eyes closed, breathing rhythmically, Zyra stood in one of the booths. She inhaled deeply and slowly placed her hands on the wooden railing. As her eyes snapped open, she jumped over the edge, somersaulted and landed in a crouch just in front of the raised area where the altar stood, the monks oblivious to her presence.

'I still gots it,' she said.

She glanced up nervously at the screens displaying the static, and then took off down the aisle of chanting monks, picking up speed and heading for the huge double doors at the front of the Temple. Her footfalls resonated on the heavy timber and iron door as she propelled herself into a back-flip, landing in another crouch. She jumped to her feet and headed back down the aisle to the altar, this time cartwheeling and somersaulting between the monks. A final jump, and she landed on the altar in front of the chanting red-robed monk, producing two throwing stars. With a double-handed throw, she flung both of them across the room. They thudded into the wood of the door, just as it began to open.

'Oi!' called Tark, poking his head through the gap and glaring at the stars. 'Watch it, will ya?'

The monks rarely did anything other than chant; their eyes were either closed or fixed firmly on the altar. The doors were not in their line of sight, so Tark could usually come and go as he pleased.

Zyra jumped off the altar and sauntered down the centre of the Temple, chanting monks on either side of her. She pulled her arms behind her back to stretch her aching muscles.

'Gots ta keep in practice,' said Zyra, as Tark stepped into the Temple.

'Yes, once you're no longer part of the game, you need to keep up your skills so they don't fade away.'

Zyra's knives were in her hands by the time the hooded man stepped into the Temple.

'It's okays,' said Tark, as he closed the Temple door, 'he's with me.'

Zyra didn't lower the knives. Her eyes were fixed on the stranger.

'Yeah,' said Tark. 'He can sees us.'

'Greetings, Zyra,' said the hooded man, bowing slightly. 'It is so very, very good to see you.'

As he took a step forward, Zyra moved to block his path, knives pointed threateningly at his throat. The man stopped. He slowly lifted his hands, palms out to show the absence of weapons, and drew back his hood.

He had long white hair, pulled back into a ponytail, a neatly trimmed beard and wild violet eyes. He smiled and the creases around his eyes deepened.

'I am here as a friend,' he said, studying Zyra.

Zyra squirmed a little under his intense gaze. There was a distinct air of familiarity about him. Zyra was certain they had never met, and yet she couldn't help feeling that she almost knew him. But that was not a reason to drop her guard.

'Who is ya?' She didn't lower her knives. 'How comes ya can sees us?'

'These days I call myself Tee,' he answered. 'I am like you. I no longer play the Designers' game. Like you, I cannot interact with anyone who is part of the game. And I have much to tell you.'

'Why shoulds we listen to ya, old man?' demanded Zyra.

Tee winced. 'Not so much with the *old*, please. I'm not even fifty.'

'Yeah?' Zyra smirked. 'Old!'

Tee sighed. 'I have information that you need and equipment that can help you.'

'He's right.' Tark took a step to stand next to Zyra. 'He's gots weapons that works on 'em static things.'

Zyra's eyes lit up and she lowered the knives a little.

Tee looked around the Temple at all the chanting monks. 'A strange place you've decided to make your home.'

'This 'ere's the only place the static leaves us alone,' explained Tark.

'Interesting.' Tee raised an eyebrow. 'Is it just the main area or the entire building?'

'The whole place,' answered Zyra.

'In that case,' said Tee. 'I don't suppose there is a quieter room in which we can talk?'

Tark and Zyra nodded. Tark led the way through the monks, to the left side of the altar. He pulled aside a drape to reveal the door leading into the vestry. Sheathing her knives, Zyra followed, watching Tee warily as she went.

Tee assessed the room quickly. 'You live back here?'

'Yeah.' Tark plonked himself down onto one of the mattresses. 'None of 'em monks eva comes back 'ere.'

'And it's quieter.' Zyra leaned up against the table, keeping her eyes glued to the stranger. 'Them monks neva shuts up. All days. All nights. Chant, chant, chant.'

Tark produced the three remaining apples he had stolen. He tossed one to Zyra, one to Tee and bit into the third.

'Is that alls ya got?' Zyra glanced at Tark.

Tark shrugged and then stuck his thumb out towards Tee. 'Gots interrupted.'

Zyra narrowed her eyes and glared at Tee. 'So it's yar fault.'

Tee held up a gloved hand in a placating gesture. 'Actually, it was a VI. What you would call a ball of static.'

Zyra took a thoughtful bite of her apple, chewed, swallowed, and then spoke. 'Okay, *old man*, ya saids ya had stuff to tells us. Well, we is listenin'. So, starts talkin'.' She pointed to the mattress next to Tark.

Tee sat himself down. 'Where to begin?'

'Starts with the static balls.' Zyra lifted herself up onto the table and sat cross-legged. She took another bite of her apple and looked down at Tark and Tee. They looked similar, she realised. Same height. Similar faces – though Tee's was lined with many extra years. Same intense, violet eyes, but Tee's seemed wilder. And while Tark slumped, Tee sat upright. He had a confidence that Tark lacked, even while sitting on an old mattress.

Tee rubbed his apple on his sleeve and looked up at Zyra. 'Always have to have the higher ground,' he muttered.

'Wot?' demanded Zyra.

'Nothing.' He looked back down at his fruit, took a deep breath and started talking. 'Okay, the static balls. You'll have noticed that they appear to be the same sort of . . . well . . . static, for want of a better word, that makes up the Interface between game environments. I assume you've been in the Interface?'

Tark and Zyra both nodded as they continued to eat.

'Well, it's as if bits of the Interface have leaked into our environment and become intent on homicide. The theory is that they are like viruses – a spreading infection. Hence the name Viral Interface, or VI for short. Every time they consume something, they gain power and grow. I've even seen one ball split into two after consuming people.'

Tark swallowed hard, the apple not wanting to go down.

'People?' Zyra had stopped eating, her fruit discarded. 'Wot people? We've neva seen 'em attack anyone other than us. No one else even seems ta notice 'em.'

'Ah, yes.' Tee looked at his apple again, shifting it from one hand to the other. 'You see, there are other people who have refused to play by the Designers' rules.'

'People likes ya?' said Tark, his eyes alight with excitement. 'People that can sees us? People we can talks ta?'

'Do you think you're the only people ever to defy the Designers? Yes, there are others. Many others. People have been breaking the rules and living without actually playing the game for as long as the game has existed.'

Tee noted the surprise in the eyes of both Tark and Zyra.

'We call ourselves Outers. We've got a community set up on the edge of this environment. We established it after the VIs showed up. Those things consumed many of us before we found a safe place. Since then, we've been working on fighting them and . . .' Tee paused for a moment, apparently lost in thought.

Tark and Zyra glanced at each other.

'You would be most welcome to join us,' Tee said, finally.

'Why shoulds we?' asked Zyra. 'We is safe 'ere.'

'Yes,' said Tee. 'Yes you are. And I'm intrigued that the VIs leave you alone while you're inside the Temple. I assume it has something to do with the Oracle. But what happens when you step outside?'

Zyra looked away. Tee reached into the small

quiver attached to his belt and pulled out a crossbow bolt, its tip static-grey.

'This bolt has been charged with the substance of the Interface.' He held it up. 'One of these can substantially weaken a VI. A second will destroy it.' He returned it to his quiver. 'And we have other weapons.' He paused. 'But there's more than that. We are working on things. Big things. Things that could shift the balance of . . . of everything.' He shrugged. 'Now, tell me about yourselves. How you discovered the Temple as a haven. How you survived.'

Tee looked expectantly from Zyra to Tark and then back to Zyra.

It was unnerving the way Tee kept watching her. There was something odd about it.

'It started with a kiss,' said Tark, smiling up at Zyra.

Tee also smiled. 'It always does.'

And suddenly it struck her. Family! It was a family resemblance. With both Tark and Tee smiling at her, it was so incredibly obvious. A sameness differentiated by years. It was like she was looking at father and son. Could that be it? Could Tee be Tark's father? She marvelled at the thought. When they had been playing the game, the notion of parents had been irrelevant, had never even crossed her mind. Yet now, here was this strange man who looked like Tark – who might be his father.

'Things changed,' continued Tark, shaking away

the smile. 'We couldn't talks ta people no more. Or touch anyone. No one could sees us. It wuz likes we wuzn't there.'

'Like ghosts,' added Zyra.

'And in a way, you are ghosts,' said Tee. 'You are no longer part of the game. You are irrelevant to anyone in the game. To them, you do not exist.'

'The weird things wuz, there were some things we couldn'ts touch,' said Tark. 'Anythin' the games people wuz usin'.'

'Yes,' agreed Tee. 'Anything that is actively in play is off limits to us.'

'And thens . . . suddenly these balls of . . . these VI things shows up.'

'And we starts runnin',' said Zyra.

'And they is chasin' us,' said Tark.

'And we is runnin' past the Temple.'

'And some dude is comin' out of its.'

'And I thinks maybes the Oracle can 'elp us,' said Zyra. 'So we runs through the closin' door.'

'But them VIs, they don't follows us,' said Tark.

They were both panting now, as if having run the whole escape all over again.

'And was the Oracle of any help?' asked Tee.

'Nah.' Tark shook his head. 'Wouldn't even talks ta us.'

'And now I can'ts even leave the Temple,' complained Zyra. 'As soon as I goes out, them things are onta me.'

'They is more wrapped up in Zyra than me,' said Tark.

'Hmmm.' Tee tugged at his beard. 'I think I can help with that.' He dug in his pockets and pulled out what looked like two stickers. 'Here. Put these on.'

'What is they?' asked Zyra, taking one and turning it over in her hands.

It was a soft, opaque plastic square with a plain white paper backing on one side.

'Medical patches that have been adapted,' he explained. 'We found a whole batch of them in a disused hospital. Each patch contains a very small amount of static from the Interface. If you look closely, you can see it.'

Zyra brought the patch up close to her face. Through the opaque plastic, she could just make out a little churning greyness.

'The patches slowly release a minute amount into your body,' continued Tee. 'Having a bit of the Interface running through you seems to confuse the VIs, hiding the wearer from them. It won't stop them if they're close by, but it will prevent them from homing in on you.'

Zyra looked suspiciously from the patch in her hand to Tee. He pulled back one sleeve to show the patch stuck to his arm, just above the wrist.

'Wear one of these and you can leave the Temple.'

Tark grabbed the second patch from Tee. Pushing back the sleeve of his tunic, he yanked off the backing paper and slapped the patch onto the underside of his wrist.

'They don't last for long,' said Tee, peeling the patch off his arm and getting a new one from his pocket. 'An hour at most.' He stuck the new one a little further up his arm. 'And don't put them in the same place twice in a row. They get itchy.' He pulled his sleeve down again and stood up, stretching. 'Now, I think it's time I took you to meet the Outers.'

He opened the door, swept back the drape and stepped through into the Temple, expecting Tark and Zyra to follow.

Zyra stared at the patch a little longer. 'Leaves the Temple, huh?' she whispered. Then she peeled the backing off her patch and stuck it onto her right cheek.

'Why'd ya do thats?' asked Tark, getting up off the mattress.

'Easier to gets it off quick, if needs be.' Zyra jumped down off the table.

Tark raised a quizzical eyebrow.

'In case he's lyin',' she explained.

'Oh.'

Zyra pointed an accusing finger at Tark. 'Ya is too trustin'. We has only just met 'im. He could be anyone.'

'Who?' Tark shrugged.

'I dunno,' Zyra snapped. 'All I is sayin', is that we needs ta be careful.'

'Okay.' Tark held up his hands defensively. 'Woteva.'

Tee stuck his head back in through the doorway, stared at Zyra, then looked over at Tark. 'Bring along any food and weapons you may have.' Again, he glanced at Zyra, before disappearing back into the Temple.

'He's a bits weird, ain't he?' Zyra stared at the door.

'This comin' froms the one with a bit of plastic stuck to 'er cheek,' said Tark, gathering up the weapons.

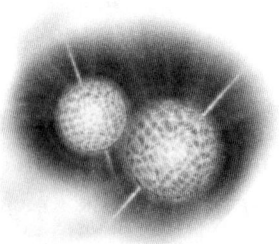

4: The Outers

Zyra glanced around nervously as she walked through the City with Tark, following the mysterious stranger taking them to meet the Outers. They had used the monks' old robes from the vestry, packing up the food and weapons into three bundles that they each carried over their shoulders.

Tee's patches seemed to be working. They were almost at the edge of the City and had not encountered a single ball of static. Yet Zyra still didn't trust him. The way he kept looking at her was unnerving. And he wasn't giving them the full story – she was sure of it. And then there was the fact that he looked so much like Tark. Could he be Tark's father?

'Oi, Tark,' Zyra whispered, shifting her pack from one shoulder to the other.

'Yeah?'

'Notice anythin' about the ways he looks?' Zyra indicated Tee.

'Nah.'

'Don't ya thinks he looks kinda familiar?' she persisted.

Tark stared intently at the back of Tee's head for a little while before answering. 'Nah.'

Zyra exhaled, long and loud. Tee glanced back at them over his shoulder and smiled. Tark smiled back.

'I don'ts trust 'im,' Zyra hissed.

'Why?' asked Tark.

'I just don'ts.' Zyra swiped at her hair, trying to keep it back. 'He coulds be leadin' us inta a trap.'

'But then why woulds he gives us the patches?' Tark tapped his cheek knowingly.

'Lullin' us inta one of 'em false senses of security.' Zyra scowled. 'Then, when we least expects it –'

Tark shook his head dismissively. 'Ya knows, sometimes ya thinks too much.'

They continued in silence, Zyra brooding over Tark's acceptance of Tee at face value. Zyra's mood was matched by the dark, overcast conditions.

Reaching the edge of the City, they passed a gang of mutants lurking in the shadows of a partially collapsed building, the glint of their mirrored shades winking from beneath their hoodies. It looked like they were rifling through the pockets of a couple of dead travellers. None of them so much as glanced in the direction of Zyra and her companions.

Zyra eyed them cautiously as she passed. If Tee could see her and Tark, she reasoned, it was possible they might encounter others who could as well – others who might not be as apparently benign as Tee.

Entering the Forest, with its thick foliage, things grew darker still. Zyra kept a close eye on Tee as he led on.

***

It felt as though they had been walking for ages, although neither Tark nor Zyra knew exactly how long. They were finding it difficult to gauge the passage of time. Since they no longer participated in the game, they had noticed that there was no regular pattern of night and day, and the sun in the sky could be anywhere at anytime. Not that they could even see the sky at the moment, with the thick canopy of trees blocking their view. Tee insisted on staying off the paths, so they had been fighting their way through dense vegetation.

It was a great relief when the Forest suddenly gave way to barren, rocky ground, which extended into mountains. At the base of the mountains, amidst the massive boulders, they could see a dark opening. That was where Tee was taking them.

As they approached, Tee motioned for them to stop. He unclipped a device from his belt. It made a musical chirruping sound when he flipped it open. He twisted a dial and lifted it to his face.

'Tee here. Let us in,' he said into the device.

A muffled voice answered.

Tee clicked it closed and hooked it back onto his

belt. The air in front of the cave entrance shimmered briefly.

'Force-field,' explained Tee as he led them to the mouth of the cave. 'Keeps the VIs out. Always be careful. Touching the field feels like having a pile of rocks dropped on your head.'

They entered the darkness and walked along the rocky passageway. As their eyes adjusted to the gloom, Tark and Zyra noticed tunnels and alcoves branching off in all directions. Continuing, they realised they were heading for a dead-end. Zyra glanced nervously at Tark.

'No need to worry,' Tee assured them.

He placed his palm against the rocky wall. Light flared beneath it and the wall melted away, revealing another passage. This time the walls were lined with sconces, each supporting a softly glowing orb.

'Magik,' breathed Zyra.

'Rechargeable batteries, actually,' corrected Tee. He looked back at Zyra. 'You can take the patch off now. You're quite safe in here.' He continued along the passage.

Zyra yanked her patch off and winced. Why did everything have to hurt? Dropping it to the ground, she glanced at Tark as he peeled the patch off his wrist.

Tee led them down the passage, through an opening and into a spacious cavern lit by large orbs hanging from stalactites. The area was filled with a mishmash of furniture, equipment and people. Tark and Zyra looked in wonder. A group of people sat on a circle of chairs and sofas in the centre of the area, deep in conversation. There was a makeshift kitchen under a rocky outcrop to their left, with a vaguely familiar man in a chef's hat bustling about, preparing food. Crates of food and drink were stacked to either side of the kitchen, forming improvised walls. To the right of the cavern was a target range with a rack of crossbows attached to the wall. A couple of younger teenagers were practising, their bolts thudding into the bullseye.

Zyra placed her pack on the ground. Tark's dropped with a clatter of weaponry. Conversations stopped, activities ceased, as heads lifted and eyes stared.

'We refer to this as our common room,' said Tee placing his pack on the ground. He stepped forward, spread his arms and turned full circle. 'Welcome to my world. The world of Outers.'

Some of the Outers smiled, some frowned. One young man raised a hand and waved. And then they all returned to what they had been doing.

Tee pointed to three openings in the far wall.

'That one leads to the sleeping quarters, that one to the storage areas, and that one . . .' He paused as a strange-looking man in a white coat emerged. 'That leads to Research.'

The new arrival laughed and clapped his hands,

then hurried towards them, his frizzy grey hair wafting about as he walked. He was very short and wore thick glasses reminiscent of goggles.

'Hello, hello, hello, hello. Welcome, welcome.' He stared at Tark and Zyra, looking them up and down carefully, his eyes darting about behind the lenses. 'So very, very, very nice to meet you. Very nice, indeed. Indeed.' He ran his fingers along his neat goatee and looked at Tee expectantly.

'Tark and Zyra, this is Professor Palimpsest.'

The professor clicked his heels and inclined his head.

'Please, please, just call me Professor,' he said eagerly, bouncing up and down on the balls of his feet. 'Indeed, yes. Just, Professor.' He turned to Tee. 'And I have made progress. Yes, yes indeed. Yes, indeed, I have. The project progresses. When you have a moment, we should talk. Yes, yes we should. Indeed. When you have a moment. Yes.'

'I'm afraid that will have to wait,' said Tee. 'I have a lot to discuss with Tark and Zyra.'

'Of course, of course.' The professor backed away. 'Indeed. Tark. Zyra. Yes. Much to discuss. Indeed. I shall leave you to it, then. Ja, ja . . . I mean, yes, yes.' And with that, he turned and walked back through the opening that led to Research.

'Weirdo,' breathed Tark, glancing at Zyra.

'He is actually rather brilliant,' said Tee. 'I don't know what we'd do without him. He designed and built the force-field that protects us. He adapted the medical patches, allowing us to move about undetected by the VIs. It was he who discovered that bolts tipped with Interface static could be used against the VIs. And now, he is working on an even greater project. Something that will hopefully shift the balance of power in our favour.'

'He talks weird,' said Tark.

'And what? You don't?' Tee looked sternly at Tark. 'Each of us has been programmed with certain stereotypical speech patterns. All the scientists have unusual speech patterns, with odd accents. He tries to overcome it. But when he was in the game, he never used Designers Paradise and he never had an avatar, so he never experienced speaking in any other way. It is difficult for him.' Tee stared at Tark for a moment, and Zyra again marvelled at their similarities. 'Unlike us, who have had avatars, who have spoken in different ways. All thievers speak the gutter speak, like you. Like I used to. But I overcame the programming. I now speak how *I* wish to speak.'

'Woteva,' said Tark, looking away.

'Both of you,' Tee continued, 'can stop the gutter speak. You just need to try. You need to want to.'

'Wot's in there?' asked Zyra, hoping to change the subject. She pointed to a small opening in the cavern wall by the kitchen.

'Ah,' said Tee, walking towards the opening. 'That one, and others like it, lead to nothing.'

'Huh?' said Tark.

'Take a look,' suggested Tee, leading them to the alcove.

Tark and Zyra could see the static nothingness of the Interface glowing in the darkness.

'Designers Paradise,' said Tark.

Tee pointed at the static. 'The Interface between the environments. These caves are right on the edge of our game environment, of what the people here call the World. It's just a peripheral place. No active play happens here, so things aren't always fully formed. There are passages that lead to the Interface. There are unstable areas.'

'So you can goes into the other places?' said Zyra. 'Like Suburbia?'

'No.' Tee shook his head. 'You can't enter another environment without a key and payment. And you have to go through the whole process of getting a path from an Oracle and making your way to Designers Paradise. We are no longer part of the game, so we cannot do that. If one of us were to enter the Interface, we would be stranded there until . . . until eventually absorbed.'

'Isn't its a bits dangerous bein' 'ere then?' asked Zyra.

'The force-field shields each of these unstable spots,' explained Tee. 'We need them. We use these unstable spots for static to tip our weapons and adapt our patches. And this area is not used in the game, which is why we have been able to set it up as a base.'

Tark sighed and shook his head slowly.

'I know it's a lot to take in,' said Tee. 'And there's still a lot more I have to tell you.' He looked from Tark to Zyra. 'A lot more.'

Zyra yawned, which set Tark off as well.

'Perhaps you should rest first,' Tee said, noticing for the first time how tired they both looked. 'How long has it been since you slept?'

'Dunno.' Tark shrugged.

'Of course.' Tee nodded knowingly. 'When you first stop playing, it can be quite disorientating. We don't have a regular passage of time in the World. Night only happens when it's needed for the game. We have clocks and calendars here to help us keep track of hours, days, months . . . years.' He pointed up to the far wall, where a digital clock showed 14:04. 'We have regular sleep periods and meal times to help maintain health and –' He stopped, looking at Tark and Zyra. 'And now I think I should be quiet and show you to your rooms.' He paused and smiled. 'Actually, one room with two beds.' He headed off. 'Follow me.'

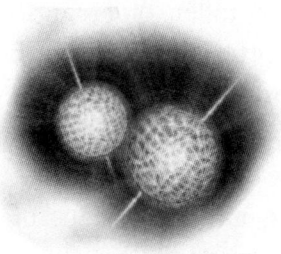

5: Familiar Faces

Tark and Zyra were following Tee again, yawning and stretching but feeling much refreshed for having slept in comfortable beds.

'I trust you slept well,' said Tee. He no longer wore his cloak. He was now in a simple pair of brown leggings and tunic, with black boots – much like Tark's outfit, only better fitting and in better condition. 'We can continue our little talk while you have something to eat. There is still so much to tell you.'

Tee led them back to the common room and towards the kitchen, where groups of Outers were eating at several long trestle tables.

'We have a Zyra,' called an excited voice from one of the tables. 'At last!'

Tark and Zyra stared, mouths agape.

'I don't believes it,' said Zyra.

'Wot's with ya?' said Tark, stalking forward. 'Is ya followin' us everywheres?'

The boy with golden hair stood up, glaring at

them. He looked taller, older and a little slimmer, with a much shorter haircut – but he was definitely Princeling Galbrath.

'I am most certainly not following you,' said the princeling, as he approached them.

'This snotling gaves us heaps of trouble in the game,' Zyra explained to Tee.

'We're not in the game now,' said the princeling, shaking his head. 'And I'm not a snotling or a princeling or any other sort of -ing, anymore. You can call me Gal.' He extended a hand, but Tark and Zyra both ignored the offer. He let his hand drop. 'I've been here amongst the Outers for about . . . oh . . . must be at least three years.'

'I don't gets it,' said Zyra, looking at Tee. 'How coulds he 'ave been 'ere that long? It's only been . . .' She struggled to think just how long it had been. 'It's only been a little while since we wuz in the game with 'im.'

'And how comes he looks different?' added Tark.

'Well,' said Tee, 'this is one of the things I have yet to explain to you. You might want to sit down for this.'

Tee indicated the stools standing by the breakfast bar in the kitchen. As he led them away, Gal watched their backs for some time before returning to his dinner.

Tark and Zyra sat down. The strangely familiar chef brought each of them an orange juice and a bowl of soup, and then returned to the large pot that bubbled away on the stove. Zyra stared after him, trying to recall where she had seen that chubby face.

'Okay,' said Tee, leaning up against the bar. 'This is going to be a little difficult to explain.' He ran a hand across his tired eyes. 'In the Designers' game there are what we call 'essential characters'. Characters who are important to the way the game develops. Characters who can make decisions. And if any of these characters ever make the decision to not play, they are replaced.'

Tark nodded, took a sip of his drink, and then looked up at Tee. 'I don't gets it.'

'About three years ago, Princeling Galbrath decided to break the rules of the Designers because he no longer wished to play their game. He became an Outer. No longer part of the game; no longer able to interact with anyone or anything in the game; able to grow older; etcetera, etcetera. Okay so far?'

'Yeah,' answered Tark and Zyra.

Tee continued. 'As soon as he became an Outer, the Designers replaced him with a new Princeling Galbrath – a Princeling Galbrath who would remain fourteen and continue to play the game. Unless, of course, he too, one day, becomes an Outer. Then he will be replaced again.'

'That's dumb,' said Zyra.

'That is the will of the Designers,' said Tee.

'Hangs on a tick,' said Tark. 'I thoughts the

Designers wuz no longer on the scene. I thoughts it wuz the Maintainers who ran things now.'

'Ah,' said Tee. 'So you've met the Maintainers. I'm afraid that they too are just characters and their control centre just another game environment.'

'Oh,' said Tark.

'I'd figured that out for meself,' said Zyra, raising her eyes to the rocky ceiling.

'Oh,' said Tark again, running a hand through his hair.

'Is that whys he looks familiar?' asked Zyra, pointing to the chef.

The chubby man turned from the pot on the stove and beamed at them. 'I used to be the Skinny Rich Dude who lived up the Hill. You can call me Chuck.' He walked over to shake hands with Tark and Zyra.

'But you is not skinny,' said Tark.

'You can put on a fair bit of weight in fourteen months.' Chuck patted his stomach. 'My being skinny was programmed into me as part of the game. It was one of the rules. I was only allowed to eat a small ration every twelve hours. I was always so damn hungry. But now that I'm an Outer, I can eat however much I want and whatever I want, anytime I want!'

'Is that whys ya left the game?' asked Zyra. 'Did ya wants ta eats more?'

'No,' said Chuck, looking away. 'It was because of Fido.'

'Fido?' asked Tark.

'My dog.'

'Ya means that furry robot thing that used ta guard yar safe?' asked Zyra.

Chuck nodded silently.

'It's been ages since I seen it,' said Zyra.

'He was killed.' Chuck's voice cracked a little. 'Every time you, or any other player, stole a key from me, you'd slip past Fido, or distract him. A couple of times you even found his off switch. But that last time.' He choked up momentarily, then swallowed hard. 'You brought a laser.'

'Oh.' Zyra looked a little dismayed.

'When I found him,' Chuck went on. 'There was no way I could put him back together. And he wasn't an essential character.'

'I . . . I is sorry,' said Zyra. 'I is not sure I even really remember it all thats well.'

'Oh.' Chuck waved his hand. 'It's okay. You were just playing the game. You had no idea what he meant to me.' He sighed, deep and heavy, and turned to face Zyra again. 'I didn't even pick up the pieces. I just went straight to the kitchen and binged on whatever food I could find. And so, I became an Outer.' He smiled half-heartedly. 'Excuse me now, I need to get back to the soup.'

Chuck turned and shuffled back to the stove, whispering, 'I still miss him.'

'I *am* sorry,' said Zyra, looking Tee in the eyes.

'I know,' he answered. 'You were playing the game. You weren't programmed to think about the people you stole from, or the consequences your actions would have. You were doing what you had been designed to do.'

'So,' said Tark. 'Does this means there is another one of me out there?'

'And me?' asked Zyra.

'Yes,' Tee answered.

'I wanna see 'em!' demanded Tark. 'Rights now!'

Tee looked thoughtfully at them, running a hand along his beard. 'All right. If we're going to head out, we need to get you some weapons first.'

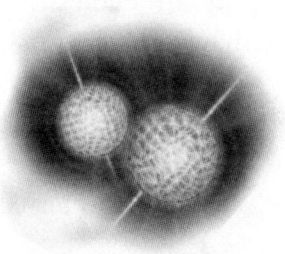

6: Tark and Zyra

Tark and Zyra watched in dumbfounded silence as Tark and Zyra planned their next robberies. The new Tark had acquired a hellfire-spear, its tip alight with a flickering blue flame, and was intending to use it to kill a dragon and win its stash of gold. The new Zyra had stolen a Designers Paradise key from the Skinny Rich Dude who lived up the Hill, and was now intending to steal another from the Cracker.

'Seen enough?' asked Tee, sitting on one of the steps leading down to the basement hideout.

'Yeah,' said Tark at the same time that Zyra said, 'No.'

'Looks at her,' said Zyra. 'Looks at her face. It's me! Except that she ain't got no pimples. And her hair is stickin' up like it's meant ta.' She turned to look at Tee. 'And she ain't gonna gets older, is she? She'll be perfect forevers.'

'For as long as she plays,' replied Tee. 'But she's trapped. Trapped in patterns of behaviour and speech. Trapped in an endless, repeating quest. Trapped by rules that stop her from getting what she really wants.'

Zyra resumed her surveillance, absently running her fingers across the pimples on her cheek.

'Is all of that really worth eternal youth?' asked Tee.

Zyra shrugged.

The new Zyra threatened the new Tark with her knives, and then turned her back on him. He stood staring at her, a pained look in his eyes.

Tark watched himself watching Zyra, recognising the longing in his own eyes.

'I've hads enough,' said Tark. 'Let's gets outta here.'

Before Tee could lead them away, the new Tark and Zyra whisked past, out of sight.

'I is glad that's over,' said Tark.

'It's never easy the first time,' admitted Tee, as he climbed the stairs. 'But you get used to the idea.'

Tark and Zyra followed.

'Can we see your replacement?' asked Zyra, thoughtfully.

'Ah, well –' Tee began as he reached the exit. He ducked back down. 'VIs,' he breathed. After waiting a few seconds he slowly peered out into the ruined City.

Tark and Zyra also cautiously looked out. The replacements were going in opposite directions, the new Tark towards the Forest and the new Zyra deeper into the City towards the Den of Thievers. Each of them was being pursued by a VI, which, of course, neither could see.

'Interesting,' said Tee. He looked back at Tark and Zyra. 'I wonder if they were expecting us to visit your replacements?'

Tark and Zyra had no opportunity to comment, for at that moment, Tee's communicator beeped. He took it out and flipped it open.

'Yes?' he said.

'Dad?' A female voice crackled breathlessly from the little speaker. 'Stine and I are under attack . . .' The voice faded away into a hissing crackle, and then slowly became audible again. '. . . whole bunch of VIs.'

'Where are you?' Tee shook the communicator and shouted into it. 'Tell me where you are.'

'. . . power station.' The communicator went dead.

'On my way,' said Tee, snapping the communicator closed. 'Change of plans.' He looked around to make sure that the VIs were far enough away, then took off through the rubble.

'Hey, whats about us?' called Zyra, staring after the departing figure.

'We betta follows,' said Tark, making a move.

'Wait,' said Zyra. 'Maybe we is betta off on our owns.'

'I don't think so.' There was a certainty in Tark's expression. 'We needs ta go now, or we is gonna lose him.'

Zyra quickly weighed up the options. 'Okay.'

They took off after Tee.

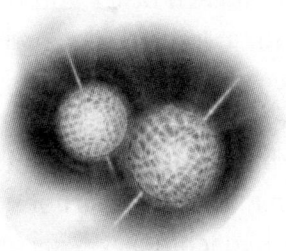

7: Hope

Spires of twisted metal rose from the concrete, windowless building. A high smokestack soared into the clouds from the centre of the structure. A chain-link fence topped with razor wire and covered in signs saying DANGER and HIGH VOLTAGE surrounded the whole area. It was an imposing building with a menacing ambience that screamed 'stay away'.

Tee slipped through a hole in the fence that enclosed the abandoned power station, Tark and Zyra not far behind him. As he ran for the door, he unhooked the crossbow from his belt. He stopped by the slightly ajar door and loaded the weapon. Without waiting for Tark and Zyra, he shouldered the door wide open and ran in.

Tark and Zyra glanced nervously at each other as they loaded their own crossbows with static-tipped bolts.

'Ready?' asked Zyra.

'No,' replied Tark.

They grinned at each other and went in.

They were in a long dark corridor lined with closed doors. Tee was already halfway down, running towards the open door at the far end, which spilled a little light into the darkness. Tark and Zyra ran after him. They burst into a cavernous, dimly-lit area full of dormant machinery – a converted factory of some sort. Huge pistons and cogs and turbines. Long, winding conveyor belts. Gigantic metal claws and enormous compressors. All frozen in inactivity. Tee was now stationary amongst the machinery, eyes darting about, searching.

They heard a scream, followed by two gunshots. The sounds echoed through the room, as if they were coming from within the machinery itself. Tee turned helplessly from one direction to another, unable to discern where the scream had originated.

BANG!

The door at the other end of the factory was thrown open as a young woman dressed in black leather came running out, trying to load a pistol. Behind her, two VIs streaked out in pursuit.

'Hope!' Tee yelled, as he ran towards her.

The woman weaved around some machinery and headed towards him, the two sizzling pursuers still behind her. Tee lifted his crossbow.

'Drop!' he yelled.

Zyra nudged Tark and they both aimed their crossbows.

The young woman threw herself to the concrete floor, rolling to one side as Tee fired. The crossbow bolt struck the first of the VIs, which immediately stopped dead as if stunned, its edges flaring and dissolving, its size decreasing. Tark and Zyra simultaneously fired at the second. Both bolts struck home and the ball of static menace burst apart, its substance dissipating into nothingness.

The young woman rolled into a crouch, slammed a new magazine into her pistol and took aim at the first VI. Tee was already reloading.

The VI recovered and charged at Tark and Zyra. They franticly reloaded their weapons, but the young woman fired first. Two successive shots, sending the VI into oblivion. Springing to her feet, she tossed her gun into the air, caught it, spun it on her finger like a Wild West gunslinger and dropped it into the holster on her belt.

'Nice,' Tark said to himself, as he watched her stride across the factory floor towards Tee, her long legs crossing the distance quickly. 'Oh, yeah. Very nice.'

Zyra elbowed him in the ribs. 'Wot?'

As she reached Tee, the young woman threw her arms around him. Tee hugged her tightly. As Tark and Zyra approached, she pulled away.

'Thanks,' she said.

Tark and Zyra stared at her, mouths agape. She was a striking figure, with a padded leather jacket and pants, dark-coloured sneakers and fingerless gloves dotted with rusty studs across the knuckles. She looked about eighteen, with long red hair tied into a ponytail and intense violet eyes . . . and a face that looked too much like Zyra's to be a coincidence.

'Ya is his daughter,' said Tark, casting an astonished glance at Tee. 'But, ya looks like Zyra.'

'My name is Hope,' she said to Tark. 'Tee is my father. My mother was –'

'Me!' Zyra blurted out.

Tee nodded.

'Huh?' Tark's astonishment turned to confusion.

'An earlier version of me,' explained Zyra. She stared at Tee. 'When I first saw ya, I thoughts ya might be Tark's old man.' She paused. 'But yar not, are ya?'

'No,' said Tee. 'The relationship is a lot closer than that.'

'Ya mean . . .' Tark's voice petered out as realisation dawned.

'My name used to be Tark,' said Tee. Sadness washed over his face and he lowered his eyes. 'But when my wife died – when *my* Zyra died – I couldn't use that name any more.'

'Ya is me.' Tark stared incredulously at Tee, then shifted his gaze to Hope. 'That means ya is my . . .' Tark's face turned red.

Hope lifted a gloved hand and waved, grinning broadly.

Tark looked to Zyra and saw the devastated expression on her face. His shoulders sagged and he slowly turned to face Tee.

'We ain't the first,' he whispered, barely able to get the words out.

'We is just copies,' said Zyra.

Their minds reeled with the revelation. To be a created character in a game was bad enough – to be a copy of a created character was completely demoralising. Zyra felt her knees weaken. She took hold of Tark's arm to steady herself. His hand grabbed onto hers and held tight, a slight tremor running through it as he drew in a long, slow breath.

'You started out as copies,' said Tee. 'As did I.' He looked at Tark and Zyra's shocked expressions. 'Yes, there were others before me. Like me, you became individuals. If the two of you were just copies, you would still be playing the game. But there will be enough time for explanations later.' Tee looked at Hope. 'Stine?'

The young woman shook her head sadly.

'Tell me what happened,' said Tee.

'We came here to salvage materials for the prof. Next thing I know, there are four of them swooping in through the door. We got one then ran.' She paused. 'Stine wasn't fast enough. I tried to help but –'

'Four!' blurted Zyra.

Hope scowled at her in annoyance.

'There were four of them VI things,' continued

Zyra, releasing her grip on Tark. 'Ya gots one at the start. We gots another two just then.'

'We need to get out of here,' said Hope.

'Wot's that?' asked Tark.

In the distance they could hear whistling.

They all turned to look at the main door as a man entered from the darkness of the corridor. Dressed all in green with a peacock feather in his cap, he walked in, casually tossing a red ruby from one hand to the other. He was whistling a happy little tune.

At that very moment the final VI came shooting through the opposite door.

'Run for the exit,' yelled Tee.

Tark, Zyra and Hope bolted. They were past the man and halfway down the corridor before they realised that Tee had not followed them. All three stopped and turned back. As they approached the door, they saw Tee running at the man in green, the VI literally a hand-span behind. Just as he was about to collide with the stranger, Tee threw himself to one side. The VI connected with the whistling man. The two entities froze in their moment of collision.

Eyes wide, Tark and Zyra watched as the man was taken apart. They had only seen bolts and throwing stars and other inanimate objects disassembled. Watching it happen to a person was another thing altogether. They knew they should be using the time to run away or fire their weapons. But they simply watched in horrified fascination, as outer layers of clothes and skin disappeared to reveal bones and muscles and internal organs, which in turn were also deleted.

As the last trace of the man vanished, the air filled with the most ghastly screeching noise they had ever heard, like worlds screaming as they are torn apart. A huge gash of light split through the air and widened to reveal the static Interface of Designers Paradise. It was as if the very fabric of their reality, their World, was being torn open to reveal the unreality behind it. The VI was sucked through the tear and then, with another ear-splitting sound, the wound healed itself, disappearing as if it had never been there.

In its place stood the man dressed in green, face blank, totally immobile. As Tee slowly got to his feet, the man in green started to move. First he tossed the ruby from one hand to the other, then he started whistling, and finally he walked off, across the factory floor and through the door at the end.

'Wot just 'appened?' asked Zyra, as Tee joined them.

'The VI took out an essential character,' explained Tee. 'I don't think they're allowed to do that. So, as well as the character being replaced, the VI was removed.'

'Okay,' said Tark slowly, trying to take it all in.

'I don't like this,' said Tee. 'There's been too many VIs about. Why?'

'We should get back to base,' suggested Hope.

'Agreed.' Tee led the way out of the building. 'Keep your eyes peeled for more of them.'

They continued into the grounds and through the hole in the fence. They had barely started their journey through the City, when Zyra glanced over her shoulder and gasped. Three VIs were flying down past the smokestack to the power station.

'Get down,' ordered Tee.

They all ducked behind a pile of rubble.

'They're searching for us,' whispered Hope.

Tee pointed to the right of the power station where another VI was making its way along a City street.

'And over there,' said Tark, indicating another two VIs on the other side.

'We need to move quickly and carefully,' Tee instructed in a hoarse whisper. 'And load up, just in case.'

Hope checked her gun as the others loaded their crossbows.

'How come ya gets one of 'em?' hissed Zyra.

'I found it,' answered Hope, flatly.

'Guns tend to be used only by inhabitants of the Hill,' explained Tee. 'They're difficult to acquire.' He raised his crossbow. 'Whereas these things are as common as muck.'

Tee led the little group from the rubble to the nearest partially standing building, then along the City streets, keeping to the shadows wherever possible. As they rounded an almost intact courthouse, they came upon another VI. Within seconds, all four had raised their weapons and fired. The VI didn't even have time to react. It burst apart with a louder than usual crack, and dissipated.

'Well, that's done it.' Hope threw her arms up and glared at Tark and Zyra. 'They'll be all over us in moments.'

'Oi,' spat Zyra. 'It ain't our fault. Ya is the one with the noisy weapon.'

Hope grunted.

In the distance they could already see a VI speeding toward them.

'Follow me,' said Zyra, taking command. Without waiting for an answer, she ran off down a side alley. Tark followed automatically.

Hope looked questioningly at her father. Tee shrugged and the two of them also followed.

Zyra led them down the alley, over a low chain-link fence, through a garbage tip and towards a scorched park, the VI in hot pursuit. They crashed through a grove of dead, blackened trees, branches falling and disintegrating into ash around them. Another two VIs joined the chase.

'We're just collecting more of them,' shouted Hope.

Zyra didn't answer, she just kept running – out of the park, through the rubble of one building and into the decaying shell of another. They emerged from the other end, dodging debris, and yet another VI joined the hunt.

Tee spotted their destination. 'Keep following her,' he called to his daughter. 'She knows what she's doing.'

They ran past more collapsed buildings before entering the graveyard, the VIs getting closer every second.

'Perfect!' panted Hope. 'We're going to die in a cemetery.'

'We ain't gonna die,' Tark shouted.

Zyra put on a burst of speed and pulled even further ahead of the others. She headed for the door at the back of the Temple of Paths. She ground to a halt, slamming her shoulder into the wall between door and window, hands fumbling with the handle. As the others caught up she flung the door open, ushering them in. They ran past her and she looked back to see the VIs almost upon her. She threw herself through the doorway at the last second, and Tark slammed the door shut.

'Oh great,' complained Hope, as she looked about. 'Now you've trapped us. You stupid –'

'Well done,' said Tee to Zyra, cutting off his daughter with an annoyed sideways glance.

Hope looked to her father as the sound of rhythmic chanting drifted into the vestry.

'The VIs can't get in here,' explained Tee. 'Don't know why. Something to do with the Oracle, I suppose.'

Hope raised a sceptical eyebrow.

At that moment, a VI appeared at the window, attempting to press itself forward. It roiled and sparked, but couldn't get beyond the glassless frame.

'See?' said Zyra, triumphantly.

'Yes, I see, thank you very much.' Hope crossed her arms and turned away, saying 'stupid gamer' under her breath.

'Gamer?' asked Tark.

'That's what we call those who play the Designers' games,' said Tee quickly.

'When we're being polite,' added Hope, with a smirk.

'So wot does ya call gamers?' Zyra challenged.

'Hope . . .' Tee's warning voice was stern.

'Zombies,' answered Hope, ignoring her father. 'Mindless creatures, not truly human, just following their programming.'

'Well, we ain't no zombies,' said Zyra. 'Nots anymore.'

'Well, you still sound like it.'

'Stop it,' demanded Tee. 'Look.'

Another VI had arrived, joining the first outside the vestry window. Long sinewy fingers of static reached out from each VI, intertwining and drawing them together. Merging into each other, they formed a larger ball of fizzling, static menace.

'I've seen them split apart, but never merge like that,' Tee murmured to himself, scratching at his beard.

The new, large VI renewed its endeavours to gain entry through the window. And it actually moved forward – just a little, but it was enough to worry the occupants.

'O-oh!' said Tark.

Tee leaned in for a closer look. 'I don't like this,' he said, forehead creasing into a frown.

Wispy tendrils of grey reached out from the edges of the VI, touching the edge of the window frame. The frame wavered as, particle by particle, it was wiped from existence.

Hope snatched her gun from its holster.

'The door,' exclaimed Zyra.

They all shifted their attention. There was a hole in the centre of the outside door – a very, very small hole, just big enough to let in a pinprick of light. That tiny glow grew and the particles of wood around the hole blistered and disappeared.

'So we're safe in here, huh?' Hope threw her arms up and paced the room. 'Yeah, safe. I feel really safe.' She brandished her gun. 'So now, we fight! Even though there are probably dozens of them out there now, and we don't stand a chance.'

'Not yet,' ordered Tee.

'I don't gets it,' said Zyra. 'They is neva been able to gets in 'ere before.'

'Yes,' said Tee, biting at his lower lip. 'But you and Hope have never been together before.'

'Wot is ya on about?' asked Tark.

'This room is not part of the Temple, proper,' said Tee, ignoring Tark's question. 'Let's get into the main building. We may have better luck in there.'

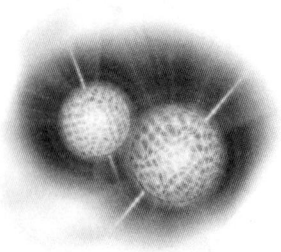

8: Sanctuary

Zyra hastily led the way into the Temple of Paths. Tark brought up the rear, shutting the door to the vestry behind them and letting the drape fall into place. The monks were doing their usual thing – kneeling, chanting and occasionally prostrating themselves.

'What if this doesn't work?' demanded Hope.

'Well, if they start to break into here, I'm banking on the monks noticing it,' said Tee. 'They're programmed to protect the Oracle at any cost.'

Tark stepped up to Tee, standing right in front of him, where he couldn't be ignored. 'Wot did's ya mean about Zyra and Hope bein' togetha?'

'I had hoped to explain this properly under better circumstances,' Tee said. 'But I suppose I'll have to tell you, now.' He indicated the step leading up to the altar behind which the red-robed monk silently knelt. 'You had better sit down.'

'More secrets,' Zyra whispered to Tark, as he

joined her. 'Why can'ts he just gives us the whole story?'

Tark and Zyra sat down together, Hope a little to the side of Zyra. Tee stood before them, addressing them as if he were making a speech.

'There is a cheat code,' began Tee.

'Actually, there's more than one,' corrected Hope.

'Yes, thank you, there is more than one,' said Tee, a hint of irritation in his voice. 'But let me deal with one thing at a time. There is a cheat code, handed down –'

'Wot's a cheat code?' asked Zyra.

'It's a code that lets you cheat,' stated Hope, flatly.

'Oh yeah, great.' Zyra glared at Hope. 'Thanks. That explains everythin'.'

'It is a code,' Tee quickly cut in, 'that contains instructions on how to circumvent the will of the Designers.'

'Instructions?' Hope's voice rose in pitch and she snorted in a half laugh.

'Yes, well,' Tee corrected. 'It's more like a series of hints. Or a prophecy. It has been passed on from Outer to Outer over many series of repeating characters. In fact, the previous Tark gave me it. And the Tark before gave him it. And so on, all the way back to the original Tark and Zyra.'

'The original us?' asked Tark.

'That's right,' said Tee. 'It seems that they may have been the first Outers. Or so we think. It was a very long time ago. No one knows how they came upon the cheat code, only that they –'

'Cuts ta the chase,' Zyra interjected. 'Wot does it says?'

'It says a lot of different things.' Tee paced about in front of the others. 'Most importantly, it says that two generations together, parent and child, a father and son or a mother and daughter, will have the ability to travel between the game worlds.'

'Anyones with a key and enough money ta gets inta Designers Paradise can gets inta other worlds,' said Tark.

'Yes, but Zyra and Hope, together, in theory, don't need a key or money,' said Tee.

The monks' chanting echoed around them, as Tee paused to let his words sink in.

'Wow!' Tark looked at Zyra with wonder in his eyes. 'Who woulds have thunk ya'd be so special.'

Zyra punched him on the shoulder, and then looked at Hope. 'How?'

'No idea,' said Hope.

'That's the problem,' Tee admitted. 'The cheat code is not very specific.'

'Well, wot does it says?' Zyra rolled her eyes and huffed. 'Exactly?'

'Exactly?' Hope mimicked. 'Zero. One. Zero. One. Zero. Zero. Zero. Zero –'

'Shuts up!' yelled Zyra. 'Wot's with ya?'

Hope produced a handheld screen from a pocket

and tossed it to Zyra. Tark leaned over and the two of them saw a stream of green numbers scrolling across the screen.

01010000 01100001 01110010 01100101
01101110 01110100 00100000 01100001 01101110
01100100 00100000 01101111 01100110 01100110
01110011 01110000 01110010 01101001 01101110
01100111 00101100 00100000 01110011 01100101
01110000 01100001 01110010 01100001 01110100
01100101 01100100 00100000 01100010 01111001
00100000 01100111 01100101 01101110 01100101
01110010 01100001 01110100 01101001 01101111
01101110 00100000 01100010 01110101 01110100
00100000 01100011 01101111 01101110 01101110
01100101 01100011 01110100 01100101 01100100
00100000 01100010 01111001 00100000 01100111
01100101 01101110 01100100 01100101 01110010
00101100 00100000 01100001 00100000 01100111
01100001 01101101 01100101 01110010 00100000
01101110 01101111 00100000 01101100 01101111
01101110 01100111 01100101 01110010 00100000
01100001 01101110 01100100 00100000 01101111
01101110 01100101 00100000 01110111 01101000
01101111 00100000 01110111 01100001 01110011
00100000 01101110 01100101 01110110 01100101
01110010 00101100 00100000 01110100 01101111
01100111 01100101 01110100 01101000 01100101
01110010 00100000 01100011 01100001 01101110
00100000 01110100 01110010 01100001 01110110

01100101 01110010 01110011 01100101 00100000
01110100 01101000 01100101 00100000 01110111
01101111 01110010 01101100 01100100 01110011
00100000 01101111 01100110 00100000 01110100
01101000 01100101 00100000 01000100 01100101
01110011 01101001 01100111 01101110 01100101
01110010 01110011 11100010 10000000 10011001
00100000 01101101 01110101 01101100 01110100
01101001 01110110 01100101 01110010 01110011
01100101 00101110 00100000 01010100 01101000
01100101 00100000 01110000 01100001 01110010
01100101 01101110 01110100 00100000 01100100
01100101 01100011 01101001 01100100 01100101
01110011 00101100 00100000 01110100 01101000
01100101 00100000 01101111 01100110 01100110
01110011 01110000 01110010 01101001 01101110
01100111 00100000 01101001 01101110 01101001
01110100 01101001 01100001 01110100 01100101
01110011 00101110

'Ya thinks ya is so clever,' said Tark, glaring at Hope. 'Ya is nuthin' but –'

'Would everyone please calm down?' Tee did not shout, but he injected his voice with authority. 'We don't have time for bickering.' He stepped forward and snatched the screen from Zyra.

'It's binary language,' he explained, tucking it away into his pouch. 'Translated, it says: "Parent and offspring, separated by generation but connected by gender, a gamer no longer and one who was never, together can traverse the worlds of the Designers' multiverse. The parent decides, the offspring initiates". I think this is why the VIs have gone on the attack. They are trying to keep Hope and Zyra from using the cheat code. Zyra is the parent, the one who is no longer a gamer, the one who can decide on a destination. Hope is the offspring, the one who never was a gamer, the one who initiates the jump from one environment to another.'

'So wots do we do?' asked Zyra.

'You and Hope need to figure that out.'

Zyra looked over at Hope, who glared back at her.

'Hangs on a tick,' Tark interjected. 'I still don't gets wot's so special about these two. Couldn't some others motha/daughta team do this jumpin'?'

'There are no other children.' Tee's voice was quiet and low. 'No Outer has ever had children before. And Zyra – *my* Zyra – died during childbirth.' He turned away. 'There is no other parent and offspring that can be teamed. We've waited a long time for a new Zyra to join us.'

'Oh,' Tark whispered.

'I was assuming we'd have plenty of time to work it all out.' Tee rubbed a hand across his tired face as he turned back to the others. 'But it seems that the VIs are determined to stop you.'

At that moment, the monks stopped chanting and raised their hooded heads.

'Look!' Tark jumped up and pointed towards the vestry door.

A pinprick of light emanated from the centre of the drape that hung in front of the door.

'Looks like we're not safe in here, either,' said Hope.

'So we better figure out how to get the two of you to jump,' said Tee.

The light from the drape intensified. Slowly, the fabric was being eaten away. The red-robed monk behind the altar rose to his feet.

'The safety of the Oracle is threatened.' His voice boomed through the Temple. He nodded to his monks and two of them got to their feet, approaching the door. The first of the monks drew a sword from beneath his robes, the second a loaded crossbow.

'They know what's going on?' said Hope to her father.

'The VIs are absorbing the door,' explained Tee. 'I was hoping the monks would perceive the threat.'

The first of the monks flung aside the drape to reveal the VI, larger than it had been before, practically filling the doorway. The second monk shot two bolts from his crossbow in quick succession. Both bolts were wiped from existence within seconds. The mass of static moved forward a few centimetres, but stopped just inside the doorway, unable to move further. It pushed forward, something forming deep within the undulating greyness – something with claws and teeth. The first monk stepped forward and lunged with his sword, plunging the blade into the heart of the writhing ball of static. Monk and static both froze. The sword was deconstructed and absorbed, the monk following suit – robes, skin, innards.

The air was torn asunder as the horrible shrieking sound echoed through the Temple.

Hope looked to her father. 'The monk was an essential character?'

'The monks are the guardians of the Temple of Paths and the Designers' Oracle.' Tee smiled at his daughter. 'They are all essential.'

'Ya knew thats would 'appen?' asked Tark.

'I suspected and hoped.'

They watched with relief as the VI was sucked into the Interface and the monk replaced. But their smiles quickly faded. With the doorway cleared, they could see that there was little left of the vestry, and that three more oversized, amalgamated VIs waited, roiling and writhing, something dark moving within each. And beyond them, blazing through the sky, dozens more were racing to join them.

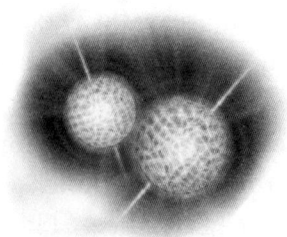

9: Jump

'Protect the Oracle,' boomed the red-robed monk's voice.

The first row of monks threw their robes off. Beneath, they were dressed in black, with a multitude of armaments attached to their belts. They drew their weapons and headed through the door. Seconds later the screeching sound of the tearing environment ripped through the Temple.

They all stared silently out through the door – Tee scratching thoughtfully at his beard; Hope nervously taking her pistol in and out of its holster; Tark and Zyra quietly holding hands.

'Wot does we do now?' Tark let go of Zyra and clutched his crossbow with both hands, his knuckles white.

'We stay put,' said Tee. 'We're safe in here for the time being. The monks will keep the VIs busy.'

'For how long?' asked Hope.

'Indefinitely, I suppose,' said Tee. 'The monks will

just keep getting replaced. And I assume there's a finite number of VIs.'

'Ya assumes,' whispered Tark.

'And if there's an endless supply of VIs,' said Hope. 'We're trapped!'

'Well, then,' said Zyra, desperately trying to keep her voice steady. 'I guess we needs ta works out how ta jump.'

'Sure,' replied Hope, throwing her arms out. 'Because it's that easy.'

There was another round of screeching from outside.

'We has gotta do sumthin',' yelled Zyra, her façade crumbling. 'Maybe all we've gotta do is thinks it. Or touch hands. Or sumthin'.'

'Oh, yeah. That would be it,' Hope yelled back, pacing in front of Zyra. 'Let's just shake hands and jump.'

'You never know,' said Tee, calming himself and looking at Hope. 'It may work. And we've got nothing to lose.'

Another row of monks threw back their robes and strode towards the door. As they passed Zyra, she thought that one of them looked at her, the corners of his mouth curving up in a slight smirk, his dark eyes twinkling. Zyra shook her head, wondering if the stress was finally getting to her. The monks resolutely headed out through the vestry door, as more screeching blared in from outside.

'If more monks is needed out there –' Tark pointed out.

'– there musts be even more of 'em VIs,' finished Zyra.

'Whats if more and more of 'em keeps coming?' asked Tark. 'Enough ta swarms over this place?'

Tee looked intently at his daughter, his eyes silently begging her cooperation.

'Fine.' Hope walked up to Zyra and stuck out her hand. 'Shake.'

Zyra reached out a hand and took Hope's.

Nothing happened.

'See.' Hope snatched her hand back and folded her arms.

'Ya ain't even tryin',' said Zyra, coming to stand face to face with Hope. 'Concentrate, will ya?'

'Don't you try telling me what to do.' Hope raised her voice. 'It's not like you're actually my mother.'

'Well, I is the closest thing ya've gots,' Zyra shouted back at her, pushing her face up to Hope's so that they were almost nose to nose. Then Zyra took a step back and turned to Tee. 'Is I enough?' she asked in an almost whisper.

Tee didn't hear. He was too busy watching the monks. Another row had just exited and the red-robed monk was now disrobing and drawing his scimitar o'light.

Zyra tapped Tee on the shoulder. 'Is I close enough ta her motha for this ta works?'

'Yes,' said Tee, his voice determined. 'I'm sure of it. Otherwise, why would the VIs be trying to keep the two of you apart?'

'Rights then,' said Zyra, making up her mind.

She strode over to Tark, pulled him to her and kissed him hard. It was all over before he even had time to respond. Tark stared after her, as Zyra strode back to Hope and placed her hands on the girl's face. 'Whetha we likes it or not, and I don'ts, I *is* ya motha.'

Hope opened her mouth to speak.

'Shuts up and thinks,' Zyra demanded. 'Thinks of getting outta here.'

Zyra closed her eyes, concentration creasing her brow. Hope sighed in resignation, closing her own. She reached up and took hold of Zyra's face. Then, simultaneously, the two of them leaned forward and touched foreheads.

To Tark and Tee's utter astonishment, they were gone.

Tark put a finger to his mouth. He felt a pang of sadness as he stared at the spot where Zyra had been. That was the first time their lips had met since their rule-breaking kiss. And now she was gone.

'I *was* right.' Tee mouthed the words silently.

The red-robed monk stalked past Tark and Tee, and out the vestry door.

'Wots about us?' Tark asked.

'Us?' Tee said. 'We fend for ourselves.'

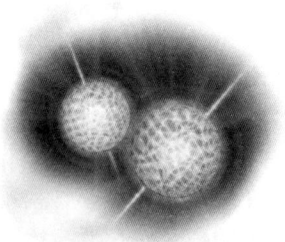

10: Legend of the Ultimate Gamer

The words Bobby's Café glowed in soft blue neon above window signage that proclaimed the best ice-cream in all of Suburbia.

'What's ice-cream?' asked Hope.

'The best thing ever,' assured Zyra, as she led the way towards the café.

'What do you do with it?'

'You eat it, of course.' Zyra pushed the door open and went in.

Wide-eyed, Hope followed.

The café was decorated in a rainbow of pastel colours – blue chairs with green vinyl cushions, yellow tables and pink walls. A large counter curved its way in front of the far wall, its orange top and blue sides standing out against the pink wall. Small round tables, each with four chairs, dotted the main area of the café. The place was deserted except for a lone man in a shabby suit sitting on a stool at the counter. He sipped at a coffee while staring down at the counter top.

Zyra led Hope to a window seat. 'You sit down and I'll go get us some ice-cream.'

Zyra headed behind the counter and disappeared through the red swinging door.

Hope stared out of the window at the impossibly perfect streetscape. It was neat and clean and like something out of a dream. The shops looked freshly painted, the street like it had just been paved, and all the passersby were dressed in their neatest best.

'Weird,' Hope murmured.

'Here you go.' Zyra plonked a white bowl onto the table in front of Hope.

Hope looked down at the contents. There were three scoops of . . . something. White, brown and pink.

'Vanilla, chocolate and strawberry,' explained Zyra as she handed her a spoon. 'Try some.' She started eating her own.

Hope tentatively used the spoon to scoop up a tiny bit of the white stuff. Slowly, she brought it up to her mouth.

'It's cold,' she exclaimed, surprised.

'Of course it is. It's frozen.' Zyra laughed. 'What do you think?'

'It's odd. But sort of okay.' Hope tried a larger spoonful, slowly rolling it around in her mouth. Then she tried the strawberry. 'This one's better.' Then she tried the chocolate. 'This one is good.' She finished the mouthful and looked up at Zyra. 'What is this place?'

'Suburbia.' Zyra gazed wistfully through the window. 'Tark and I came here whenever we had the money and keys to get into Designers Paradise.'

'Zombies,' said Hope.

'Would you stop it!' Zyra slammed her spoon down on the table. 'We are stuck with each other. So let's just make the best of it.'

Hope looked down at her bowl of ice-cream without answering.

'Like it or not,' Zyra continued, 'I'm your mother.'

'You are not!' Hope growled through gritted teeth, violet eyes flaring with rage.

Zyra stared into those eyes – Tark's eyes – and calmed herself. 'I am. And I'm not. It's weird, I know. Let's just accept that we need each other. Okay?'

Hope's anger subsided and she let out a long breath. 'Okay.' She had another spoonful of the chocolate and looked up. 'So, why this environment?'

'It's peaceful,' said Zyra. 'It's nice. No one trying to kill us. No one to steal from. It was a chance for us to not be us – to be Tina Burrows and John Hayes, instead.'

'You became different people?'

'Avatars.' Zyra thoughtfully tugged at one of her earrings. 'We looked different. We spoke differently. I guess we became who we really wanted to be.'

'Hmmm.' Hope finished off the chocolate ice-cream, eyeing the other two flavours suspiciously. 'You still look like you, now. But you're speaking normally. You've lost that stupid gutter speak.' She loaded up a spoonful of strawberry. 'How come?'

'Oh! Well.' Zyra looked down at her own ice-cream. 'This is how people speak here. It's how I speak when I'm here.' She quickly put a spoonful of vanilla ice-cream into her mouth.

'Yeah,' said Hope. 'But we're not playing the game. No one can see or hear us. So, why the change?'

'I dunno,' said Zyra, reverting to her usual way of speaking. ''Cause I wants ta.'

'Oh, great.' Hope dropped her spoon into the bowl. 'You know, it sounds really dumb when you talk like that. You sound like you're stupid.' She looked away from Zyra. 'And you're not.'

They sat in silence for a while, eating their ice-cream, their black and red leather outfits incongruous amongst the pastel dreaminess of the Suburban café.

Zyra finished her ice-cream and sighed. 'So, what are we going to do now that we're here?'

Hope pushed her bowl away, the vanilla uneaten. 'We start our mission.'

'We have a mission?' asked Zyra.

'Didn't my father tell you anything?' Hope snorted. 'No, I suppose he didn't have time. We need to find the Ultimate Gamer.'

'I barely even met your father before the VIs started chasing us around,' Zyra explained. 'I don't know very much at all.'

'What a surprise,' sniped Hope.

'Don't get all smartypants with me,' said Zyra. 'Just explain this mission and who the Ultimate Gamer is.'

'Sorry.' Hope glanced down at the yellow tabletop, then back up at Zyra. 'Here it is in a nutshell. There's a legend. It's been passed down from Outer to Outer in another cheat code. There's supposed to be this gamer who is outside the control of the Designers. He plays whatever he wants in whatever environment he chooses and he doesn't have to play by the rules. The Ultimate Gamer makes up his own rules.'

'Wow.'

'There's more. This is the main bit. The reason my father wants us to find him.' Hope paused. 'According to the legend, the Ultimate Gamer has the ultimate cheat code – the ability to leave the game environments and go into the real world.'

'Double wow.'

'I always thought that it was just a story.' Hope shrugged. 'But then, I thought the mother/daughter cheat code was a load of crock as well.'

'So how do we find this Ultimate Gamer?' asked Zyra.

'I don't know,' admitted Hope.

'You're kidding?'

Hope slowly shook her head, a little embarrassed under Zyra's glare.

The door behind the counter banged open and a waitress walked through. She wore a pale blue dress with a white apron and a name tag that said

'Heidi'. She placed another cup of coffee in front of the man sitting at the counter. The man didn't even acknowledge her. He just pushed his old cup aside and picked up the new one, sipping loudly. The waitress continued around the counter and walked straight towards Zyra and Hope's table. She took an order booklet from her apron pocket as she stopped at their table.

Zyra and Hope glanced at each other and then back at the waitress. She tore a page out of the booklet and placed it on the table between Zyra and Hope. Then she put the booklet away, turned around and walked off.

'Hey!' shouted Zyra, after her. 'Can you see us?'

The waitress gave no sign of having heard her as she made her way behind the counter and through the door.

Zyra looked back at Hope and then at the paper face down on the table. She reached forward and turned it over, then snatched her hand back.

I'll find you.

The two of them stared at the paper and the words, written in bold red, looking almost like blood. There was something ominous about the simple statement. Zyra shivered and looked over at Hope.

'So,' said Zyra, breaking the silence. 'We just sit here and wait for this Ultimate Gamer to show up.'

'No,' said Hope, alarm in her voice as she pointed out the window.

Zyra looked out to see a VI heading down the street. She reached for the crossbow on her belt.

'No,' Hope said again. 'It might not have seen us. It could just be looking for us. Best if we just quietly jump again.'

'Back to the Temple of Paths?' asked Zyra.

'No,' said Hope. 'Try another environment.'

'Suburbia is where Tark and I always came. It's the only one I can picture in my mind.'

'You never went anywhere else?' asked Hope.

'We were forced into a space battle once,' she explained. 'And there was the Maintainers' Control Centre. Other than that, we only ever went into another environment one time.'

'Take us there,' demanded Hope.

'It was a long time ago,' said Zyra. 'I can't really picture it very well.'

'Well, you'd better try,' said Hope. 'I think we've been spotted.'

Zyra glanced out the window again. The VI was speeding towards them, another two VIs in the distance coming to join the first.

Zyra took hold of Hope's face and closed her eyes.

The man in the shabby suit looked up.

And they were gone.

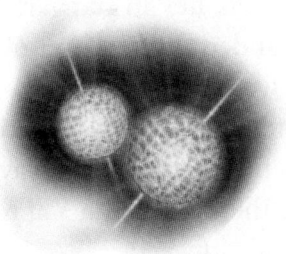

11: Left Behind

The red-robed monk strode back through the doorway, the rest of the monks streaming in after him. He approached the altar, put his robe back on and knelt down.

'Let us pray,' his voice boomed through the Temple. 'And give praise to the Designers.'

The monks all knelt in their places and resumed chanting as if nothing had happened.

Tark tentatively approached the doorway and peered out. The vestry was completely gone. He stepped out. There wasn't a VI in sight.

'Wot's 'appened?' he asked.

'They're gone,' said Tee, following Tark outside. 'We're obviously not important.'

'So where has they gone?' Tark looked at Tee with worried eyes, fearing the answer.

'They're probably after Zyra and Hope,' said Tee. 'Which means we're on the right track. Zyra and Hope, and their ability to travel, must be a threat.'

'Zyra! Ya've puts her in danger! We've gotta do sumthin',' demanded Tark, a hint of desperation in his voice. 'Can we gets her back?'

Tee looked steadily at Tark. 'Where she and Hope go is up to them. We have no way of contacting them or getting them back. They'll return once they complete their mission.'

'They has a mission?' Tark's eyes widened. 'Wot mission?' He took a step towards Tee, eyes narrowing. 'Why didn't ya tells us?'

'Well, I haven't really had the time to fill you in on everything,' explained Tee. 'Things have been moving pretty quickly. I had intended to explain everything to you and Zyra bit by bit, so as not to overload you with information. I suppose I should just tell you everything, now.'

'No,' said Tark. 'Ya can tells me later. Right now, we needs ta gets 'em static balls back 'ere.' He paced back and forth in front of Tee. 'We need ta distract 'em. Keeps 'em away from Zyra.'

'Well,' said Tee. 'There may be a way. Professor Palimpsest has been working on a little something that might help.'

'Somethin' else ya haven't told us about?' growled Tark. 'Maybe Zyra wuz rights not ta trust ya?'

'Oh, Tark.' There was a sadness in Tee's eyes. 'How can you not trust me? I'm the closest thing you have to family. In a way, I *am* you.'

'Ya is not me!' Tark jabbed a finger at Tee's chest.

'I is not ya. Ya is ya. And I is me.' Tark lowered his hand. 'Ya said it before – I is not a copy of ya no more.'

Tee stared back silently.

'Zyra didn't trusts ya,' Tark continued. 'But I has no choice. Ya is me only link ta her. Ya is me only chance ta keeps her safe. So comes on, let's see wot yar professor's been workin' on.'

Tark walked off. 'And it's betta be good,' he muttered under his breath.

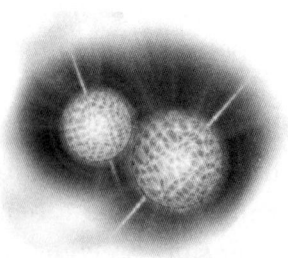

12: Now What?

'Keeps yaself close behinds me,' said Zyra.

'Oh, you're not going to start that again,' said Hope. 'Just because we're no longer in Suburbia does not mean you have to start talking like an idiot again.'

Zyra grunted and pushed forward.

'What is this place, anyway?' Hope struggled through thick undergrowth, branches catching at her clothes, scratching her hands and face.

'The only otha place we has eva –' Zyra stopped herself and tried again. 'The only other game environment Tark and I ever visited.'

'Quite a contrast to Suburbia,' said Hope.

'Yep,' Zyra agreed. 'That's why we never came back to this place. That's why we just stuck to Suburbia.'

'So you don't like jungles?'

'It's not that.' The jungle thinned, taking less effort to move through. 'It's just that Suburbia was safe.'

'And this place isn't?' asked Hope, as she followed Zyra out into a clearing.

'Not if you're playing the game.' Now that they were out in the open, Zyra pointed up towards the treetops in the distance. Hope's eyes widened as she saw the gigantic creature.

'That's a Tyrannosaurus Rex,' said Zyra. 'T-Rex for short. We studied them at school in Suburbia. One of the most dangerous dinosaurs.'

A herd of smaller creatures came running out of the jungle to their left. They were about half Zyra's height, with green scaly skin and a sparse covering of orange feathers across their backs. They stopped in the clearing, sniffing the air and looking around. The T-Rex let out an ear-splitting roar. The new arrivals took off, making panicked yelping cries, heading for Zyra and Hope. They split into two groups and ran to either side of the girls, disappearing into the jungle behind them.

The T-Rex charged. The ground shook with every step it took. Zyra and Hope ducked for cover, even though they knew it could not see them. The massive dinosaur crashed through the jungle, flattening trees as it went. It burst into the clearing. With another roar, it continued its pursuit. Hope screamed as the creature's foot thundered down within arm's length of her. And then it was gone. Zyra and Hope peered out from their hiding places and staggered into the clearing. They collapsed onto the grass.

'Okay,' panted Hope. 'I can see why you didn't want to come back here.'

There was another roar, more distant this time, and they looked up to see the dinosaur's head rear up above the jungle canopy as it devoured one of the smaller creatures. And then it was gone again.

'I is so glad —' Zyra closed her eyes momentarily. 'I *am* so glad I'm not a gamer anymore.'

'I'm glad I never was,' said Hope.

The girls lay on the grass for a minute longer, calming themselves. Finally, Zyra sat up and lifted her sleeve to check her patch. 'I think this thing is empty.'

Hope checked her own patch. 'Mine too.'

'How long to do you think we have?' asked Zyra. 'Before the VIs find us again?'

'Your guess is as good as mine,' admitted Hope. 'But I think we should be ready to jump at a moment's notice.'

'So where do you want to go when we jump next?' asked Zyra. 'Suburbia, the control centre, the space battle environment or home? That's all I know. I can't visualise anywhere else.'

'None of those,' said Hope. 'The VIs found us pretty quick in Suburbia and I think it's because they expected us to go there. If you've only been in this Dinosaur land once, then it may take them longer to find us.' She grinned. 'But if we go somewhere you've never been? Well, there are hundreds of environments for them to search through.'

'Yeah, great,' said Zyra. 'How do we get there?'

Hope sat up. 'How about you just try and think of something that could be associated with an environment?'

Zyra frowned.

'Come on,' said Hope. 'You're the one who got this world-jumping happening in the first place by simply trying it. So try this. Think of something.'

'Like what?'

'I don't know.' Hope looked around. 'Think of the absence of jungle.' She laughed, and looked up at the sky where grey storm clouds were gathering. 'Think of blue skies and sunny days.'

A white horse came galloping out from the jungle on the opposite side of the clearing. It stopped to munch on some grass.

'Horses,' said Hope. 'This environment has horses?'

Zyra gaped at the animal. 'Um . . . I don't think that's a horse.'

The creature looked up from its feeding and stared directly at them. Protruding from its forehead was a long, white, spiralling horn.

'That's a unicorn,' whispered Zyra. 'In a dinosaur environment? Odd. And I think it can see us.'

'Impossible,' said Hope. 'We're not part of the game. It doesn't know we're here.'

'Then why's it looking straight at us?'

'It's not,' said Hope. 'It must be looking at the jungle behind us.'

She twisted around to look behind them, searching the vegetation for something that might have attracted the unicorn's attention.

'I dunno,' said Zyra, nervously glancing over her shoulder. 'It appears to be looking at us. Maybe we should jump now, just in case.'

'Okay,' said Zyra. 'Start thinking.'

'Maybe I should try and think about the Ultimate Gamer,' suggested Zyra, the unicorn momentarily forgotten. 'Then maybe we'll go to wherever he is?'

'Great idea!' said Hope.

'Except, I don't know what he looks like. Or even if he is a he.' Zyra paused. 'Maybe I should just try and think of gamers in general? Or playing the game? Or, I dunno.'

'Whatever you think of, better do it fast,' said Hope. 'We've got company.'

Zyra looked up to see two VIs zooming over the treetops.

'That was quick,' said Zyra. 'I thought you said it would take them longer.'

'What do I know?' said Hope. 'I was just guessing. And hoping.'

'Right.' Zyra took hold of Hope's face and closed her eyes. Hope closed her eyes and put her hands on Zyra's face.

'Gamers,' whispered Zyra.

They jumped.

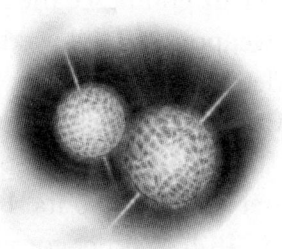

13: The Thing in the Cave

'So ya thinks this Ultimate Gamer can gets ya out of the game?' said Tark to Tee, as they walked through the Forest.

'If he even exists,' said Tee.

Tark stopped dead. 'Ya means he mights not?'

'Well, yes,' admitted Tee. 'It's a legend. It may well just be a story. Hope certainly doesn't believe there's any such person.'

Tark's expression turned dark. 'So all this danger that ya've puts us through mights be for nuthin'? And whats about Zyra?'

'I'm *hoping* that the Ultimate Gamer exists,' said Tee. 'And given that the VIs seem intent on keeping Zyra and Hope apart, I think there's a pretty good chance he does.'

'Rights,' said Tark, taking a deep breath and looking away. 'So whats da we do now?'

'I want to show you something.' Tee loaded his crossbow and started off through the Forest again. 'It's just over here.'

'I thoughts we wuz gonna see the professor?' Tark loaded his own weapon and followed.

'Just a short detour.'

'Nuthin' is eva straightforwards with ya.'

Tee huffed. 'It's not even a proper dialect, you know. That gutter speak of yours. It's really rather poorly designed. It has little consistency and no purpose other than to designate you as street trash.'

Tark ignored him.

They walked for another few minutes before emerging from the trees. They stepped out into a clearing, beyond which was a cliff face with a cave. A VI hovered in front of the cave opening. Tee shot it. Tark automatically followed suit with a second bolt, dispatching it completely.

'In there.' Tee pointed at the mouth of the cave.

Tark peered into the gloom. Inside was a writhing mass of static, bigger than even the combined VIs, with a darkness in its depths that made Tark think of rats and refuse and decaying things. It roiled and writhed and changed its shape, taking on one vague form after another. Most passed by too quickly for Tark to discern, but he did see teeth and claws – he was certain of that – and a gaping emptiness that might have been a ravenous mouth.

Tark took a step forward, mesmerised by the whirling static, hoping to get a better view, but Tee put a hand on his shoulder.

'There's a force-field on the cave, to keep that

thing in there,' said Tee. 'The professor set it up shortly after we discovered it.'

'Wot is it?' asked Tark, unable to take his eyes from the undulating mass.

'We're not sure,' admitted Tee. 'It's linked to the VIs. I think it controls them in some way. Or maybe it's their source of power. We're just not sure.' He frowned in thought. 'There's usually at least three or four VIs hanging around here. Sometimes they even try to get through the force-field.'

Tark looked around cautiously. 'I don't sees any more.'

'Neither do I.' Tee took a deep breath. 'Which makes me think that now might be a good time to attack it, while most of the VIs are busy chasing Hope and Zyra. We might be able to destroy it, or damage it, or, at the very least, lure some of the VIs back here and away from Hope and Zyra.'

'Rights.' Tark lifted his crossbow and eagerly reached into his quiver for a bolt. 'Anythin' ta helps Zyra.'

'They won't do any good,' said Tee. 'It's much too strong.'

'Gotta try,' said Tark, licking his dry lips. 'Gotta try and helps Zyra.'

Tee gently put a hand onto Tark's crossbow. 'It won't help her if we let that thing escape.'

'So how does we attacks it?' demanded Tark.

'Ah,' said Tee raising his hand. 'That's why we

need to talk to Professor Palimpsest.'

'Okay.' Tark lowered his crossbow but continued to stare at the static creature, a determined look on his face. 'Then whys did ya waste time comin' 'ere?'

'I wanted you to see it,' explained Tee. 'I wanted you to know what we are up against.'

'Rights,' said Tark. 'Well, I has seen it.'

As they left, Tark thought he heard humming coming from the cave – harsh, guttural, yet tuneful.

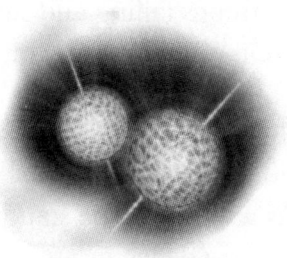

14: Brains!

Zyra and Hope were standing in a deserted city street. They looked around to see a couple of smashed shop windows and a door left swinging in the wind. Litter danced in the breeze and an eerie silence prevailed.

As Zyra gazed about, she thought that perhaps this was what the City in her environment may have looked like before it crumbled to its current state. She had to remind herself that the City had always been destroyed – it had been designed to be so. Just like this city had most likely been designed to be deserted.

'What's that?' Hope pointed to a dark stain on the pavement beneath their feet.

Zyra crouched down and ran a hand over the concrete. She looked up at Hope. 'Blood.'

'Great,' said Hope. 'Just where have you brought us?'

'I don't know.'

A pained, bloodcurdling scream echoed in the distance.

'I don't think I like this place,' said Hope.

The sound of things falling and smashing pierced the air. Gunshots and more frantic screaming followed this.

'What exactly were you thinking about when we jumped?' asked Hope.

'I don't thinks we shoulds be standin' out heres in the open,' said Zyra, deflecting the question. 'We is too vulnerable.'

Zyra headed for the nearest doorway and stood under the awning in the shadows.

'Now you're just trying to distract me with that stupid gutter speak,' said Hope, coming to join her. 'Which means whatever you thought of, it wasn't good.'

'I was trying to get us to the Ultimate Gamer,' said Zyra. 'I was rushing because of the VIs and thinking of gamers and then, well, I remembered what you called gamers and –'

A loud moan from inside the shop made both the girls jump out from the doorway.

'Oh no,' said Hope. 'You didn't.'

The door smashed open and someone came shuffling out. Actually, it was more of a something – something that had once been human, but was no more. It had wide, bloodshot eyes and thin, peeling lips drawn back from blackened, rotting teeth. It drooled a foul-smelling ichor as it made a horrible moaning sound. Lank, filthy hair hung down around its face. Its flesh was stretched tight around its skull, with strips hanging loose and flapping about as it lurched forward.

'You've got to be kidding!' shouted Hope. 'You thought about zombies. Of all the stupid, ridiculous things to –'

'Hey, don't blame me,' Zyra yelled back. 'You is the one who first mentioned them!'

More creatures came lurching out from the shop, staggering between the girls like a line of lemmings, and heading down the street. In the distance they saw someone duck out from another shop, look towards them, and take off in the opposite direction.

'Brains!'

Zyra and Hope whirled back to the doorway. As the row of zombies stumbled along, one of them stepped out of line towards Zyra. It held a dismembered, human arm in its hand, blood still dripping from the end. And it was looking straight at her.

'One of 'em is looking at me,' called Zyra.

'It can't see you,' shouted Hope over the top of the shuffling undead. She tried to calm her voice. 'It's just looking at the street behind you, that's all. It can't see you. It doesn't know we're here. We are not playing the game.'

'Are you trying to convince me?' Zyra's voice was a bit shaky, although more controlled than Hope's. 'Or yourself?'

'Brains!' The zombie smiled a revolting, blackened, rotting grin, and tossed the arm at Zyra. It landed at her feet. 'Fresh, brains,' it moaned, reaching out towards her.

Zyra unhooked the crossbow from her belt. Within seconds it was loaded and aimed at the approaching monstrosity.

Hope tried to get through the column of moving corpses. But they were part of the game and she was not, and she could not touch them, let alone push through them.

'Girl brains,' intoned the solo zombie, as it lurched towards Zyra.

'It can definitely see me,' yelled Zyra, firing her crossbow at point-blank range. The bolt thudded into the creature's forehead, right between the eyes. Blood trickled down its nose as it staggered back. Regaining its footing, it reeled forward, making a grab for Zyra.

'Run,' cried Hope.

Zyra threw the crossbow at it and took off. The weapon thudded into its chest and fell to the ground as the creature gave chase with a surprisingly speedy shuffling run.

The last of the undead came out of the shop and Hope was finally able to get past, sprinting after Zyra and her pursuer.

Zyra turned a corner and found herself in a dead-end alley. Turning back, she saw the creature closing in. Hope appeared behind it, firing her pistol. Little blooms of red blossomed on the zombie's tattered clothing. It turned on Hope. Zyra grabbed the opportunity, launching herself at it, kicking out with her booted feet. She caught it on the back of its neck. There was a sickening snap and it fell to the ground as Zyra continued over it. She ran to Hope and flung her arms around her.

And they jumped.

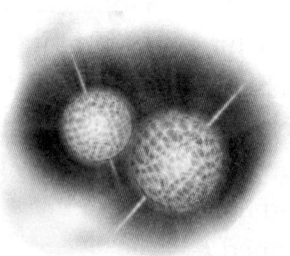

15: IDD

'It is complete,' announced Professor Palimpsest. 'The Interface Discharge Device. Yes. Or the IDD. Yes, yes.'

He proudly displayed the cobbled together apparatus. It looked like a weird cross between a gun and a syringe. Held together with wires and electrical tape, its large glass cylinder was filled with static from the Interface.

'It's been a long time coming.' Tee took hold of it, feeling the weight of it in his hands.

'I know. Yes, yes, yes.' The professor nodded. 'As you see, the syringe is filled with the substance of the Interface. When you press the trigger, a portion is released along an electric discharge, which is generated here.' He tapped the rubber-enclosed chamber beneath the syringe. 'Here, here.'

'Hangs on a tick,' interrupted Tark. 'Aren't the VI things made of the same staticy stuff as wots in there?' He pointed to the syringe. 'Won't ya just kinda be feedin' 'em?'

The professor looked shocked. 'No,' he said slowly, moving his head from one side to the other. 'No. No.' He shook his head more vigorously, as if dispelling unwanted doubts. 'No, no, no, no, no. As far as I can tell, the VIs are some form of virus. Their make-up is similar to the static substance of the Interface between environments – but it is a corrupted version. The pure substance from the Interface should counteract the viral aspects of the VIs. Should. Yes. Should.'

'Like when the VI absorption of an essential character causes a rift to the Interface?' said Tee. 'Which always ends in the destruction of the VI.'

'Indeed. Indeed.' The professor smiled, relief clear on his face. 'Yes, yes, yes. That is it. Yes. Should.'

The lack of conviction was plain upon Tark's face. 'Should? As far as ya knows?'

'Well . . . um . . . ah . . .' Palimpsest fumbled for words. 'It is all theory. Yes. But.' He held up a finger and waggled it at Tark. 'But, but. Theory based on prior experience and observation. Yes. All our anti-VI developments have been based on this theory. Yes. The patches. Yes. The bolts. Yes.' He smiled triumphantly. 'They work. Yes. As shall the IDD. Yes, yes.'

Tark glowered, still not entirely convinced.

The professor shifted his attention back to the IDD before Tark had the chance to raise any more questions. He indicated a dial on the side of the rubber-enclosed chamber. 'This controls the amount of electricity that is discharged and therefore the amount of Interface substance that is released and fired at the target. I am not sure how much will be needed, so I have set it to the lowest setting. You will need to try it and adjust the setting if necessary. Yes, yes. Adjust.'

'Why nots just bumps up the setting now?' asked Tark.

'Brim-full of questions, aren't we? Hmm.' The professor fiddled with the buttons on his lab coat, his lips curling into a tight smile. 'The higher the setting, the fewer times the IDD may be fired.'

'Oh.' Tark stared at the professor.

'Oh, indeed,' said the professor. 'Indeed, indeed. At its lowest setting, you have fifty shots. At its highest, you have ten.'

'What if the highest setting isn't high enough?' asked Tee.

'Ah. Yes.' The professor scratched at his goatee. 'Yes. I did take that possibility into account. There is an override switch.' He slid aside a panel next to the dial on the IDD, revealing a small switch. 'That will override the settings and empty the remaining contents in one continuous discharge.'

'Whats if —' Tark began.

'If it doesn't work?' Palimpsest cut him off. 'Run, run, run!'

As Tark and Tee turned to leave the professor's

workshop, they found Gal standing in the doorway, arms crossed over his chest.

'I should be going instead of Tark,' he said.

Tee shook his head. 'I need Tark with me.'

'Why?' demanded Gal. 'Because he's potentially you?' He narrowed his eyes. 'Well, he isn't yet. He hasn't been an Outer for long and we don't know if he's trustworthy.' He strode into the workshop. 'But here you are, showing him the latest research, taking him on a vital mission.'

'I trust him,' said Tee, looking at Tark rather than at Gal. 'I trust him with my life.'

'I don't.' Gal paced back to the doorway.

'Fine,' said Tee. 'Then you can come with us.'

Tee clapped Tark reassuringly on the back before walking out. Tark followed, murmuring 'Snotling', as he passed Gal.

Gal glared at their backs for some time before also leaving.

Professor Palimpsest shook his head slowly. 'It doesn't really matter who goes. No. So long as they can run, run, run.'

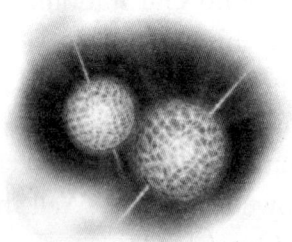

16: No-man's-land

'That was impossible.' Hope's voice was shaky. She was still holding onto Zyra.

'Yeah, well, it happened, didn't it?' Zyra did her best to keep her voice steady. 'You can let go of me now.'

'It shouldn't have happened,' said Hope, releasing Zyra, and holstering her pistol. 'That thing shouldn't have been able to see us.'

'So you keep saying.' Zyra stared at Hope. 'I think that unicorn was looking at us, too. I think you're wrong. I think some people and creatures can see us.'

Hope looked away and gazed around at their surroundings. 'Where are we?'

'No idea!' Zyra also looked around.

They were standing in mud. It was a flat, featureless landscape, with sodden ground as far as the eye could see. The sky was dark and brooding with storm clouds blocking out the sun. In the dim light, Zyra and Hope saw twisted masses of barbed wire. An icy wind blew across the desolate terrain, making them shiver despite their warm clothing.

'What were you thinking when we jumped?' asked Hope.

'Nothing,' said Zyra, trudging off to examine the nearest coil of barbed wire. 'I wasn't thinking of any place. I was just scared. I thought we were about to die.' She pushed at the wire with a booted foot.

'So we're nowhere?' Hope slowly turned 360 degrees, carefully surveying the landscape. A bitter wind howled past. 'Some sort of war zone?'

'No-man's-land!' Zyra cried, looking up from the wire. 'The unoccupied area of ground between enemy trenches during a war.'

She caught a glimpse of movement from the corner of her eye and spun around.

'What's wrong?' asked Hope.

'Not sure,' answered Zyra, eyes searching the terrain. All was still. 'I thought I saw something.' She took a few steps and then spotted a shape lying in the mud. A rifle. Eyes lighting up, she moved to get it.

'Where are you going?' demanded Hope. 'Don't go too far. We don't want to get separated.'

Moving quickly, Zyra bent down to scoop up the rifle. But all she got was a handful of mud. She tried again, but her fingers were unable to grasp it.

'Damn!'

When Zyra straightened up, she again saw movement. Was the ground moving? No! It was a soldier. Covered in muck from head to toe, he crawled slowly across the desolate battlefield towards her. Reaching out a camouflaged hand, he grasped the rifle and continued, blending in with his surrounds. Zyra blinked in disbelief. When she looked back, she could no longer locate the soldier.

'We're in the middle of something,' called Zyra.

'No kidding,' said Hope.

'I just saw a gamer.'

A distant rumble interrupted them.

Hope looked towards Zyra. 'Thunder?'

A high-pitched, whining, whistling sound filled the air.

'I don't think so,' yelled Zyra.

A patch of ground a couple of hundred metres from them erupted in a massive explosion. Both girls ducked as dirt rained down on them.

'I don't like this place,' complained Hope, still cowering.

'Me neither,' agreed Zyra, standing and trying to brush mud from her coat. She looked in the direction of the explosion and thought she could see mangled bodies. She shuddered and turned back towards Hope. 'Well, let's not stay here.'

Another rumble filled the air, closer this time, and the whistling sound started again. They looked up to see something streaking through the sky towards them.

'Run!' yelled Zyra.

They sprinted as the ground between them erupted, the force of the explosion propelling them through the air.

Zyra hit the ground, face down.

Hope landed on her side, dazed. Before she had time to recover, hands appeared from a concealed trench, grasped her and pulled her down.

Zyra sat up, coughing and spitting mud. She wiped the muck from her face as best she could and looked around. It was as before – an endless, featureless terrain, broken only by the occasional coil of barbed wire. She could discern no movement.

She called out. 'Hope!'

There was no answer.

'Hope!'

Zyra struggled to her feet, weighed down by her sodden clothing. Her precious coat was barely recognisable as red. She looked about, trying to spot Hope.

'Hope!' she called out again, an edge of panic to her voice.

Where could she be? Zyra's mind raced through possibilities as she frantically scanned the surroundings. Was Hope tangled in barbed wire? she wondered. Swallowed up by the mud? Torn apart by the explosion? Dying? Already dead?

Zyra staggered back to where the shell had hit, her coat flapping about her legs, and examined the muddy crater. No sign of her friend. She stumbled on in the direction she thought Hope had been thrown, eyes scouring the ground as she went. Up ahead, she saw a person-sized depression in the ground. She crouched down to examine it closer. It looked like she had landed there and then . . . rolled away. But where to?

Zyra stood up, stepped over the depression, and fell into a trench – face down in the muck, again. She howled with rage as she sat up, wiping her face and spitting dirt. Opening her eyes, she looked straight up the barrel of a rifle. A man in a grey uniform clutched the weapon. He had a voluminous coat wrapped around him and a gas mask over his face.

Zyra scrambled backwards until her back pressed against the trench's damp wall.

'Up!' The soldier's voice was muffled by the mask, giving it a slurred, inhuman sound.

Zyra scrambled to her feet, eyes darting about, looking for an escape route. To one side, the trench curved away concealing what lay further along. To the other side, the muddy walls seemed to stretch on forever behind the soldier. Above, the walls looked improbably high.

'Move!' The soldier nudged her with the end of the rifle.

Zyra grabbed the barrel and yanked. The soldier stumbled, releasing the rifle as he fell to his knees. Theatrically twirling the firearm around like a baton, Zyra quickly had it pointed at the soldier.

The man tilted his masked face up at her. Zyra found it unnerving being unable to see his eyes.

'Takes ya mask off!'

The soldier got to his feet and unhurriedly took

hold of the rifle's barrel. With a display of amazing strength he swung both the rifle and Zyra around to the other side of the trench, slamming her into the wall.

Zyra gasped as the breath was knocked out of her. Overcoming the initial shock, she fired the rifle into the man's chest.

He didn't move. He kept hold of the rifle and continued to stare at her with his blank, masked face. Was there even a face behind that mask? wondered Zyra. She had a sudden vision of cold, featureless flesh, moulded to the shape of the gas mask.

She fired a second time.

The soldier swung her around again, throwing her into the opposite wall before yanking the rifle from her hands. Turning it around, he nudged her with the end of the barrel.

'Move!' he grunted.

Zyra had no option. She began edging her way along the curve of the trench. It twisted and turned, making it impossible to see what was beyond each bend. The soldier kept poking her in the back with the rifle and barking, 'Move!'

Zyra wasn't sure how long they walked. The walls curved one way and then the other and then back again in a featureless, endless tunnel of mud.

Finally, the trench widened out and around the bend was an oblong-shaped area, like a little muddy room, a ceiling of grey stormy clouds rolling past overhead. And in the centre, Hope was slumped in a chair, arms and legs bound tightly, her head hanging down, eyes closed. Beside her was a second chair, empty and waiting.

'Sit!' The soldier pointed to the chair with the rifle.

Zyra stumbled over to the chair and sat down, looking across at Hope, relieved to see the rise and fall of her chest. She was alive. Zyra sat back, glad that she had not been left alone. She looked up at the soldier to see a red blaze behind the eye pieces of his mask.

'Magik!' Zyra's surprise doubled when she felt movement at her hands and feet. Ropes were coiling themselves around her ankles and wrists. She struggled, but they tightened.

The soldier grunted and walked behind the chairs. Zyra turned as far as she could, frantically trying to keep him in view. He strode over to a door in the far wall that Zyra had not noticed. It was dark and wooden and old, set directly into the mud. It couldn't possibly lead anywhere. The soldier yanked the door open and disappeared into the blackness beyond.

The moment the door closed Zyra looked back at Hope.

'Wake up,' she hissed. 'Hope! Wake up!'

Hope didn't stir. Zyra stared at her, looking for signs of life. Was she breathing? Had she imagined the movement of her chest earlier? Was she dead?

'She is not dead.' The cold voice spoke from behind her.

Zyra twisted her head to see a man closing the door. He was tall, with a long face and skinny, skeletal fingers. He wore a grey uniform, like the soldier, but his was neater and better fitting, tailored for him rather than off the rack. The jacket had a high collar with a little gold insignia that Zyra couldn't make out. There were stripes on the epaulettes, signifying rank, although she didn't know what rank. And pinned to the front of the jacket were several medals. Despite the bitter cold, he did not wear a coat.

The man slowly circled Zyra and Hope, his ridiculously clean shoes making a clicking sound with each step, even though he was walking on mud.

'You are worried for your friend with the hopeful name?' He spoke in clipped, measured tones, as if each word was an effort to pronounce. 'This is excellent.'

He stopped in front of Zyra. 'She is unharmed. She is but sleeping. If you wish her to remain unharmed, you will answer my questions. You understand?'

Zyra nodded.

'Superb.'

Zyra stared at the man, studying every contour of his face, every element of his uniform. Who was he? Why was it she could interact with him? Was he some sort of Outer?

'My perception is unclouded,' said the officer.

'Huh?'

'Most entities are unable to perceive you,' he

explained. 'You do not partake in the game, so the perception of you has been clouded. But my ability to perceive is beyond most others.' He paused. 'Now, keeping your friend in mind, it is time for you to answer my questions. What are you doing here?'

For a moment, Zyra was tempted to answer 'sitting in a chair', but the officer's cold stare dispelled that thought.

'Nothing, really,' said Zyra, trying to think of a way to explain herself. 'We're sort of just passing through. Travelling.'

'Really? In a war zone?' The officer's face betrayed no emotion. 'For what purpose do you *travel*?'

Zyra glanced at Hope.

'Yes.' The officer gave a single, slight nod. 'Her life depends upon your answers.'

Zyra closed her eyes for a moment, deciding that she had better tell the truth. 'We're looking for someone.'

'Outstanding! And who might that be?'

'Well, not that it will mean anything to you, but we're looking for the Ultimate Gamer.'

'Ah. Now we reach the heart of the matter.' Again, the single, slight nod. 'How do you propose to find this Ultimate Gamer?'

'I don't know,' Zyra admitted. 'We got a note from him saying that he would find us.'

'But he has not.'

'No.' Zyra lowered her head and her voice.

'And yet you still . . . hope.'

Zyra looked towards Hope, slumped in her chair. 'Yes.'

'Excellent. Hope makes for more determined gamers. Thus, a more interesting game.'

'Huh?' Zyra looked back up at the officer.

'What is it that you wish of him? This Ultimate Gamer.'

'Um . . . help?'

'He will not give it.' The officer shook his head.

Zyra's eyes lit up. 'You know about the Ultimate Gamer?'

'Oh yes.'

'Do you know where he is?'

'Oh yes.' The officer smiled for the first time, albeit a strained, difficult smile that looked as if it might crack the dry, papery skin of his face. 'He is here.' He turned to Hope. 'You may wake.'

Hope's eyes snapped open and her head jerked up. 'Zyra.'

'Hope.'

'We've found him,' she gasped.

'You are much mistaken,' said the officer. 'It is I who have found you.'

'You mean you're –' began Zyra.

'Indeed.' He clicked his heels together and inclined his head. 'He who you have been seeking.'

'But –' Zyra looked from the officer to Hope. 'Are you sure?'

'It's got to be him,' said Hope.

Zyra stared at the officer, eyes wide. Could this really be the Ultimate Gamer? And if so, why did he have them tied up in a wartime trench? Bemusement turned to annoyance.

'So, what's all this about then?' demanded Zyra, struggling to loosen the ropes.

'It is all but a game.' The officer spread his arms and smiled as if he really meant it. 'Have you not worked that out yet?'

'We're sick of games,' spat Zyra, getting one hand free. 'We want out.' She pointed to the officer. 'And you can help us.'

'What makes you think that I would help you?'

'Look out!' called Hope.

Zyra twisted in her chair, looking one way and then the other. And then she followed Hope's upturned, panicked gaze. Above the trench, the sky was filled with VIs, all converging on the trench. So many that they blocked out the clouds, making the sky look like a giant television screen tuned to a dead channel.

'The game is not over yet!' The officer laughed, high and staccato, sounding as if it was a painful thing to do. 'Not by a long shot.'

He slowly raised a hand, snapped his fingers and their surroundings were gone.

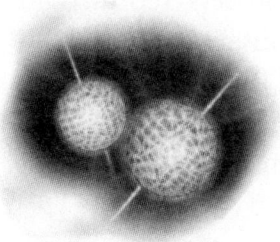

17: Testing

'Ready?' asked Tee.

'Yep,' answered Tark.

Gal simply grunted.

They were each leaning up against tree trunks, Tark and Gal holding loaded double crossbows, Tee cradling the IDD in his arms.

Tee straightened up. 'Let's go, then.'

The three of them stepped around the trees and out into the clearing, weapons at the ready. Two VIs hovered by the entrance to the cave, just outside the force-field. Tark and Tee both fired.

Tark's bolt temporarily immobilised one of the VIs.

A bright crackle of electricity arced from the tip of the IDD like a lightning strike to the other VI. It expanded as it absorbed the discharge, a balloon ready to burst. Tee was about to up the intensity and try again, when the expanded VI vanished in a blaze of light.

Tee fired again as the second VI regained its

mobility. The process repeated itself – lightning, expansion, and disappearance.

'Works,' said Tark.

'Seems to,' agreed Tee.

'Shoulds we tries it on that thing?' Tark pointed to the cave.

Inside the cave, the static moved and bubbled, indistinct images whirling and eddying within it.

'I'd like to try it out on a few more VIs first,' said Tee. 'See what happens if I up the intensity a little.'

'Here's your chance,' said Gal, looking up to the sky.

Five VIs were speeding in their direction. Tark and Gal aimed their crossbows.

'Leave them to me,' instructed Tee, as he turned the dial on the IDD up one notch and fired. As the lightning struck the middle VI, the other four changed direction, splitting into two groups. The middle VI swelled, more so than the first two victims of the IDD, and vanished in a burst of light.

Tark and Gal watched anxiously as the remaining VIs combined themselves into two larger spheres and resumed their attack. Tee increased the intensity again, and fired at one and then the other.

'That thing in there is getting bigger,' warned Gal, gazing into the cave.

'Time ta shoots it?' said Tark, eagerly.

Malevolent eyes stared out from the depths of the fluctuating mass.

'Not yet.' Tee was staring up at the sky, a sheen of sweat across his brow.

Dozens of VIs were bearing down on them, flying in arrow formation, ready to strike.

'Crap!' said Gal, raising his crossbow. 'We can't handle so many of them.'

'Damn the Designers,' Tark swore. 'Wots we gonna do now?'

'There's only one thing I can think of.' Tee spun the dial on the IDD up to ten, aimed at the foremost VI and pulled the trigger.

Lightning arced through the sky, striking the leading VI. The formation froze in the air as the electricity crackled between them, creating linking tendrils of power and spreading the substance of the Interface. The VIs expanded simultaneously, merging as they grew.

The thing in the cave roiled and screeched, as if crying out in rage and pain.

And then the VIs were gone in one blinding crescendo of brightness. Tee squinted and held up a hand to shield his eyes, but watched every second of the destruction, while Tark and Gal turned away.

Dozens of dark, piercing eyes stared out from the cave at the three of them.

'Now?' asked Tark.

'Now!' Tee yelled.

Tark took out the remote control device that operated the force-field and pressed a button. The barrier shimmered as it switched off.

Teeth gnashed and claws extended. The mass of static launched itself at them. Tee fired.

The creature howled as the electrical charge carried the pure substance of the Interface into it, slamming it back into the cave. It writhed and burbled as if trying to take on a definite shape. And it grew. A face formed within its depths. A face with evil eyes and a sharp-toothed grin.

'Weak.' The word emerged from the cave as a deep rumble, like the sound of a devastating earthquake.

Without hesitation, Tee slid back the panel, hit the override and fired again. He fought to hold onto the IDD as the power blazed forth.

'Not enough!' The words rumbled over the crackling sound of the discharge.

The energy finally dissipated, the IDD spent and useless. The face in the static solidified. It was huge and ugly and misshapen, its hate-filled eyes fixed on Tark.

'Reactivate the force-field,' ordered Tee.

Tark didn't move. He stood, transfixed by the swirling static eyes.

'Force-field!' yelled Gal.

'Zyra,' the creature rumbled, baring its fangs.

Tark dropped the control. He lifted his crossbow and fired both bolts. Laughter rumbled from the cave. Gal jumped forward, scooped up the control and activated the force-field.

A shimmer flickered across the mouth of the cave. The mass of sizzling malevolence grew, surging forward and pressing itself against the barrier. Sparks filled the air as claws formed in the static, scrabbling against the invisible screen.

'You idiot!' growled Gal.

'Zyra,' Tark whispered, dropping his crossbow. 'It said Zyra.'

'So what?' Gal turned to Tee. 'You see? You can't trust him. He's a risk.'

'Zyra's in danger.' Tark's voice was louder and higher as he grabbed Gal by his tunic, shaking him. 'We've gotta do somethin'.'

Tee placed a hand on his shoulder. 'We're trying.'

'It ain't good enough.' Tark released Gal and shook Tee's hand off. He stared down at the ground where a small animal was burrowing its way up out of the earth.

'He's unstable,' hissed Gal.

Tark glared up at Gal, ready to yell back. His words caught in his throat as his eyes widened. He bent down, yanked the little burrowing creature out of its hole and threw it at Gal.

Gal yelped and ducked. The creature slammed into the VI that had appeared behind Gal. The menacing grey ball halted as it took apart the hapless animal, giving Tee just enough time to drop the IDD, snatch the crossbow from his belt, load and fire it. Meanwhile, Tark scooped up his own crossbow from where he had dropped it, loaded it and quickly fired.

'Unstable,' muttered Tark, as the VI dispersed.

Gal straightened up and managed to mumble a half-hearted, 'Thanks.'

'Come on.' Tee picked up the IDD, gently took Tark's arm and led him away, leaving Gal to follow.

As the three of them headed off into the Forest, they could hear the creature laughing and screeching as it tried to break through the barrier that confined it.

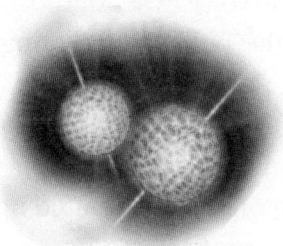

18: Pinball

Darkness!

'Hope?'

'Yeah, I'm here. I'm fine! You?'

'I'm okay, too,' said Zyra. 'I'm not tied up anymore.'

'Me neither,' said Hope. 'What happened?'

'I think we jumped.'

'How?'

'The Ultimate Gamer, I suppose.'

Ding! Ding! Ding!

The sound of a bell echoed through the darkness.

'Correct!' A voice boomed around them. 'Time to play.' It was not a voice Zyra or Hope had heard before. 'Our first contestant today is a has-been gamer who used to play as a thief in the game environment known as the World. When not questing she would escape to the environment of Suburbia.'

A bright spotlight shone down on Zyra. She raised a hand to shield her eyes.

'Zyra is sixteen years old, and has been for quite

some time.' The voice was loud, brash and overly enthusiastic to the point of irritating. 'Her hobbies include knifing people, flinging her throwing stars and admiring how she looks when she twirls around in her red leather coat.'

'What's going on?' Zyra shouted up into the light.

'Our second contestant is a born non-gamer,' said the voice, ignoring Zyra.

A bright spotlight illuminated Hope.

'Hope is eighteen years old, making her technically older than her kindasorta mother, Zyra. Her hobbies include dissing cheat codes, thinking she knows better than everyone else and making snarky comments.'

'Who are you?' shouted Hope.

'And at the controls . . .'

A drum roll echoed around Zyra and Hope before another spotlight broke through the darkness. High above them, a figure floated in a pool of light. Dressed in multi-coloured robes and wearing a ridiculously large conical hat with a propeller on top, he spun around and bowed low.

'Give it up for . . . the Pinball Wizard!'

Applause thundered through the darkness as the Pinball Wizard blew kisses to his adoring, unseen fans.

'What happened to the Ultimate Gamer?' asked Zyra, looking across at Hope.

'Still playing,' shouted the Pinball Wizard as he waved at them.

'Today's game is pinball,' announced the disembodied voice.

Lights blazed and the darkness was extinguished. Squinting through the glare, Zyra and Hope took in their surroundings. They were inside a massive pinball machine, standing in the middle of the lower level, surrounded by lights and bells and colours. Behind them, two more levels rose up like a construction site, ramps going up and down, more lights and bells, all draped in a candy-striped circus tent. In front of them, an enormous plastic clown's face, mouth open in an unnaturally wide grin, stared at them with vacant eyes. Lurid, psychedelic patterns covered every surface, with distorted paintings of jugglers, fire-eaters and circus freaks glaring out at them from posters plastered haphazardly around the game.

'I've got a bad feeling about this,' said Zyra.

'Really?' Hope glared at Zyra. 'No kidding?'

'Maybe we should jump now?' suggested Zyra.

'No way!' said Hope. 'We need the Ultimate Gamer.'

'Ready girls?' cried the Pinball Wizard, as a wand appeared in his hand. 'Time to play . . . Sudden Death Pinball!'

'Sudden death?' said Zyra and Hope together.

'That's right girls,' said the Pinball Wizard. 'If you get hit by a ball, you die. Suddenly.'

Loud, discordant carnival music blared around them.

The Pinball Wizard waved his wand theatrically and pointed it at the clown face, which proceeded to spit out a large silver ball, aimed straight at them.

Zyra and Hope jumped in opposite directions, the ball rolling between them.

'Well, that wasn't too hard,' said Hope.

'Run!' yelled Zyra.

The ball hit a rubber ring around one of the bells, making it clang, and bounce back towards Hope, accelerating. Coloured lights winked on and off around them, the music speeding up.

Hope dodged the ball and ran for the nearest ramp. Zyra took off for the opposite side. The ball hit another bell and bounced to the far end of the game, gaining speed.

The Pinball Wizard laughed and waved his wand, the clown face spitting out another three balls. One of the balls nestled itself into a depression in the floor, while the other two pursued Zyra and Hope up each ramp. The ball in the depression was then launched into the air, landing on the top level.

Zyra and Hope met on the second level and bolted for the centre ramp leading to the top. The two balls pursuing them collided, exploding in a shower of sparks. Reaching the top level, the girls only had one ball to avoid, which seemed easy enough. But as they scurried across the checkerboard pattern on the floor, the ball suddenly disappeared through a trapdoor.

Zyra and Hope froze, three of the black squares

opening up in front of them. As they gazed around, trapdoors opened randomly across the floor.

'Back to the ramp,' yelled Zyra. Before she could move, the floor beneath her gave way. She landed hard on the second level. Seconds later Hope was sprawled a metre to her right. They scrambled to their feet.

The ball that had fallen down before was still ricocheting about the second level, flung from one bell to another. Zyra dashed for the closest down ramp and Hope followed.

They emerged onto the lower level in time to see a horde of balls gushing from the clown's mouth. The Pinball Wizard's laughter echoed from above.

'I've got an idea,' said Zyra.

Lights and bells went off around them. Zyra ran towards the back corner on the lower level, dodging balls as she went. Hope followed.

Nestled behind one of the ramps was a bell surrounded by a rubber ring. It was relatively out of the way, and unlikely to get many balls. Zyra drew one of her knives and got to work on the rubber.

'Warn me if any balls head this way,' she ordered Hope.

'There's one now,' called Hope, immediately.

The girls ran to one side. The ball hit the rubber ring, sounding the bell, and bounced off. Zyra quickly returned to cutting.

'Almost got it.'

'Another one,' called Hope.

Again, they jumped back out of the way. The ball hit the rubber ring; the bell rang, the ball rolled off and the piece of rubber snapped, flicking across the pinball game to the front of the lower level. It came to rest a short distance from the plastic clown face.

'Come on,' called Zyra, dodging, jumping and sidestepping balls as she raced forward.

Reaching the strip of rubber, she picked it up, handing one side to Hope and keeping hold of the other.

'Stretch it,' she said. 'It's like a giant rubber band. We've got to use this to fling a ball up at the Pinhead Wizard.'

As another ball came shooting from the clown's mouth, the girls stretched the strip of rubber. The ball hit the centre of it. The girls gave it some slack and then pulled with all their might, trying to angle it upwards.

The ball went sailing up into the air straight for the Pinball Wizard. He ducked to one side, spinning a full 360 degrees.

A siren blared. The balls froze, the bells stopped ringing and the coloured lights winked out. A bright pink neon sign above the circus tent flashed.

TILT! TILT! TILT!

'Cheaters!' The Pinball Wizard's voice screeched through the darkness.

The *TILT* sign blew up in a burst of colour, raining sparks and shards of glass down onto the levels below. Around Zyra and Hope the light globes started bursting one by one, the flashes lighting up the pinball game with a strobing effect.

Above the game, orange flames engulfed the Pinball Wizard as he spun through the air screaming. Eyes burning with rage, he pointed at the girls.

'Cheaters!' he screamed again. The flames grew, flaring out from him in all directions, as he swooped down towards Zyra and Hope.

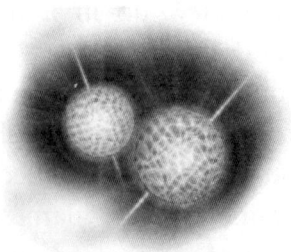

19: Reload

'Very interesting,' said Professor Palimpsest, scratching at his goatee. 'Yes, yes, yes. Very, very.'

'Interestin'?' spluttered Tark, gesturing wildly with his hands. 'Ya stupid machine hads no effect on that . . . that thing in the cave. And all ya gots ta says is *interestin'*?'

Tee put a hand on Tark's shoulder to calm him down, and then looked at the professor. 'So, what do you think happened?'

'Well . . . well, well, well. I would surmise that the discharge was not strong enough. Yes, that is what I would surmise.'

'I used the override,' said Tee.

'Yeah,' added Tark. 'Maybe it just don't works.'

'You said my IDD was effective against the VIs.' The professor nodded. 'Yes, yes, yes. Therefore it should work on the manifestation in the cave. It is considerably more powerful and therefore needs a larger discharge. You had already expended a reasonable amount of the substance on the VIs. Yes.'

'So, you think a full discharge should do it?' asked Tee.

The professor shrugged. 'It seems . . . possible.'

Tark snorted.

'Well, now. If I had more time, I could perhaps attach a second syringe,' said the professor. 'Thus expanding the storage capacity. Yes.'

'How much time?' asked Tee.

'Oh dear, dear, dear.' The professor scratched at his head with one hand, stroking his goatee with the other. 'I would have to take the whole thing apart. So well . . . let me think . . . at least, well, at least six or seven hours, I should think. Maybe more. Yes, maybe, maybe. Yes.'

'Yar kiddin'?' huffed Tark.

'Oh, no, no, no,' assured the professor. 'I do not . . . kid. No.'

'We don't have the time,' said Tee. 'That thing looked like it was going to break through the forcefield. We need to hit it ASAP, and we need to hit it hard.'

'Yeah,' agreed Tark. 'Hard enough ta thrash the static outs of it.'

'Well, well, we can charge it up right now.' The professor took the IDD from Tee and carried it over to a workbench. Picking up a cable, he plugged it into the back of the IDD.

'Wot's that?' asked Tark.

'Ahhh.' The professor's eyes lit up. 'I have set up a link to an exposed area of Interface.' He pointed to a cable. One end snaked across the ground into an alcove in the rock wall at the back of the workshop. The other end was plugged into a box with switches on the workbench. Numerous cables protruded from the box, leading to a variety of devices, including the IDD.

'This is like a switchboard,' explained the professor. 'From here I charge the bolts and the patches. Yes. As well as any experimental devices, such as the IDD.'

He flicked a switch on the box and the IDD filled with static. Then the professor disconnected it.

'The very best of luck.' The professor handed the weapon to Tee. 'Luck, luck.'

'We needs more than luck,' complained Tark. 'We needs betta weapons. I is gonna has to keep the VIs busy while Tee blasts the thing in the cave.'

'Well, well, well.' A smile crept across the professor's face. 'I have been working on other things.'

'Oh yeah?' A glimmer of interest entered Tark's eyes. 'Anythin' I coulds use?'

'Hmmm.' The professor raised a bushy eyebrow. 'Perhaps, perhaps, perhaps. You would need, I presume, something that can fire more than one shot?'

'Yeah.'

'Preferably rapid fire?'

'Yeah,' Tark said again, with greater enthusiasm.

The professor held up a hand. 'Now, I have not, as yet, had the opportunity to properly conduct all the necessary testing, but –'

'Yeah?' Tark raised his hands impatiently.

The professor shuffled off to a locker at the other end of his workshop and came back carrying a large weapon that vaguely resembled an oversized double crossbow. Its centre was encased in a black cylinder with a series of holes at one end. At the business end, a long metal tube protruded.

'A rapid fire crossbow,' announced the professor. He handed it to Tark, who turned the weapon over, examining it from all sides, disappointment evident on his face.

'Don't ya has any guns?' asked Tark. 'Likes the one Hope wuz usin'? Or maybe one of them machineguns the guards on the Hill has?'

'No guns, I'm afraid. No, no,' lamented the professor.

'I already told you,' added Tee. 'We only have what we can salvage.'

'Yeah, yeah, I knows,' grumbled Tark. 'But it ain't fair.'

'You will have to make do with what is at hand,' said the professor, patting the experimental crossbow that Tark was holding. 'This is loaded with forty-two bolts and has a double action, twin-bow setup. Yes. As the first bow fires, its release of power not only launches a bolt, but also pulls back the second bow, ready for firing, whilst also slotting the next bolt in place.'

Tark looked at the weapon with respect.

'Pull the trigger and release, to fire one bolt.

Keep the trigger pulled back for rapid fire. It has the capacity, in theory, to fire one bolt per second. I will be endeavouring to increase the speed for the next model. Yes.'

'In theory?' Tark's enthusiasm wavered.

'Yes, yes, yes, in theory. As I said, it requires further testing.' The professor smiled. 'Testing, testing, testing. That is what you shall be doing.'

'And how do you reload?' asked Tee.

'Ah.' The professor's forehead creased into a heavy frown. 'That is the drawback. It must be returned here for reloading. Yes! Here!'

'Forty-two is enough,' Tark said.

'Thanks, Prof,' said Tee. 'Come on, Tark, we need to get going.'

The professor watched them leave. He removed his glasses and rubbed at his worried eyes. 'Dear, oh dear,' he whispered to himself. 'Dear, dear, dear.'

***

'You're taking him with you again?' Gal shook his head incredulously.

'It's my decision,' said Tee flatly.

'Your decisions are becoming questionable,' said Gal. 'Tark's too erratic and too new to all this.'

'And if you're going to question every decision I make, then I can't risk taking you along.'

Gal folded his arms and glared. 'He can't even speak properly.'

'I can, if I so choose,' Tark piped up, scowling at

Gal. 'I am not the moron you think me to be. I have spent a great deal of my gaming life in Suburbia as John Hayes, speaking the way supposedly normal people do. I can speak like you if I want to. But I is choosin' ta speaks like me.'

Gal stared at him in stunned silence.

'Get a team together,' said Tee, stifling a smirk. 'We leave in five minutes.'

Gal huffed and left.

'He hates me,' said Tark, glaring at Gal's back.

'He's not all that fond of me either,' said Tee. 'It's a hangover from the game. Our characters were often opponents.'

Tark remembered how he stole the sword o'light from Princeling Galbrath.

'Now,' said Tee, his expression turning grave. 'Are you okay to come along? I need to know I can trust you.'

'Ya can,' assured Tark. 'Last time wuz . . . it's just that I is worried about Zyra. I knows she can takes care of 'erself. But . . .'

'I know,' said Tee. 'It's hard when you know she's in danger and there's not much you can do.'

'I feels helpless. Useless.'

'And you've never felt like that before,' said Tee. 'Playing the game was a lot easier, wasn't it? There was no helplessness. There was always something to do, one more trick to try. If Zyra was in danger, you'd just go and help her and save the day. But now you can't, and there are all these feelings that go along with it.' Tee managed a wan smile. 'I know exactly how you feel. But I don't have a magik solution. It doesn't get any easier. You just learn to cope. And there's always . . . hope.'

Tark looked into Tee's violet eyes – tired, surrounded by creases, yet still sparkling with life. They were his own. 'Let's go.'

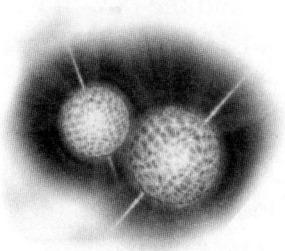

20: Bobby

Flames consumed the Pinball Wizard as he landed. Zyra and Hope had to shield their eyes and faces from the heat.

'It's okay,' someone said. 'You can look now.'

Slowly, Zyra and Hope turned around.

The Pinball Wizard was gone. In his place was a young boy. He was dressed in white trainers, faded blue jeans and a red T-shirt with the slogan *Born to Play* emblazoned across it. He didn't look a day over twelve.

'Sorry about that.' He ran a hand through his light brown curls. 'Sometimes I get a bit carried away.'

Zyra and Hope stood gaping at the boy.

'You mean –' began Hope.

'You're –' started Zyra.

'Yep.' The boy nodded shyly. 'I'm the Ultimate Gamer.'

'But,' said Zyra. 'What about the guy in the uniform?'

'That was me,' said the boy. 'It was an avatar.'

'Oh.' Zyra and Hope looked at each other and then back at the boy.

'My name's Bobby.' The boy stuck his hands in his pockets and kicked at the floor with his feet. 'You guys have been looking for me.'

'Yeah,' said Hope. 'We have.'

Zyra and Hope looked at each other again.

'It's just that . . .' Zyra looked back at Bobby. 'You're not what we expected.'

'What did you expect?' asked Bobby.

'Don't know,' admitted Zyra. 'But you're not it.'

'Oh, well,' said Bobby. 'I guess I should go then.'

'No!' Zyra and Hope called out together.

'Please don't go,' said Hope. 'We really do want to talk to you.'

'Yeah, I know.' A mischievous twinkle shone in the boy's eyes. 'So what do you want to talk about?'

'Is the cheat code real?' asked Hope.

'Yep.'

'You have the key to the real world? A way out of here?'

'Yep.'

Hope glanced at Zyra.

'If you've got a way out of here, why are you still here?' asked Zyra.

'I don't want to go,' answered Bobby, matter-of-factly.

'What?' said Hope, frowning.

'Why not?' demanded Zyra.

'Why would I want to leave?' He looked at them as if they were complete idiots. 'I want to play.'

'You want to play?' Hope said slowly, as if grappling with the concept.

'Yeah! Play!' There was excitement in his voice. 'I am the Ultimate Gamer, you know. In here, I can control things. I can play whatever I want to play, how I want to play it. It's awesome! I love it!' His cheeks were flushed with exhilaration, accentuating his freckles. 'Every time I win, it's like . . . it's like the best feeling ever.' He paused and frowned. 'I don't even know what's out there, beyond the game.'

'Freedom,' said Zyra.

'What do you do with freedom when you get it?' asked Bobby.

Neither Zyra nor Hope knew how to respond to that.

'I've got all the freedom I want,' explained Bobby. 'The freedom to play. The freedom to win. The freedom to be whoever I want to be.'

'So, is this really you?' asked Zyra, tentatively.

'Good question.' Bobby smirked, sucking his lower lip into his mouth, eyes widening with mock innocence.

'Well, how about a good answer?' prompted Zyra.

'You're not very patient, are you?' Bobby's body stretched and his clothes darkened. His voice took on a cold, calculated tone. 'Patience is a virtue. Or so I have been reliably informed.'

Zyra and Hope took a step back as the cold eyes of the officer bore down on them.

'Perhaps this is the real me?' The officer stretched out his arms to either side. 'Perhaps not.'

The officer was no longer there. In his place was the soldier with the gasmask.

'Better?'

A soft red glow emanated from behind the lens of the gasmask, and then the man in the shabby suit from the café replaced the soldier. He took off his hat, revealing lank, greasy hair, and took a bow.

'Bobby's Café,' whispered Hope.

'Yeah, all right,' said Zyra, putting her hands on her hips. 'We get the picture.'

'Do you?' The man's hair thinned, and a clump of it fell out. His clothes aged, becoming threadbare and torn. His eyes sank into his skull as his face thinned, the flesh stretching taut. Sores blossomed on his skin. 'Do you really?' He smiled, revealing rotting, broken teeth. Black ichor oozed from the corners of his mouth as he moaned. 'Brains.'

Hope took a step back, but Zyra stood her ground. 'Yes,' she insisted. 'Really. We do understand what you're capable of. We get it. And you've been following us around.'

The zombie grabbed the bottom edges of his jacket and flipped it up over his head. As he did so, it turned into a cowl, which extended itself into robes. 'Om. Oh-but-I-am-hav-ing-so-much-fun. Om,' chanted the monk.

'Oh, would you stop being so childish,' snapped Zyra. 'And before you go changing again, we know you were probably the unicorn as well.'

'Fine!' Bobby stood before them once more. A horn grew from the middle of his forehead, spiralling out.

'Enough!' yelled Zyra.

'Spoilsport,' grumbled Bobby, the horn gone.

'Okay,' said Hope. 'So you can take on pretty much any shape you like?'

'There's almost unlimited avatars to choose from,' said Bobby.

'So, is it because you don't like who you really are, that you have to pretend to be other people?' asked Zyra.

'Oh, like you can talk – Tina!' Bobby stuck his hands in his pockets again, hunching his shoulders.

'That was different,' said Zyra. She folded her arms defensively. 'I was playing the game without knowing it. It was what I was supposed to do. Now that I know it was all just a game, I don't play and I don't take on avatars. But you – you don't have to.'

'I want to,' said Bobby. 'It's fun. Sometimes I even play as me. But it's more fun to use an avatar. I like to play. And I love to win.'

'Don't you get tired of winning all the time?' asked Zyra.

'I don't always win.' A dark expression washed over Bobby's face.

'Really?'

'Sudden Death Pinball doesn't count because you CHEATED!' Bobby lowered his voice again. 'I've lost before . . . once.'

Bobby glared at Zyra, hatred filling his eyes as his body shimmered and bloated, expanding like a balloon. Folds of flesh gathered around his neck and chin as his clothes enlarged to meet the needs of his growing body, transforming into a dark suit and red cravat.

Zyra gasped.

The Fat Man lumbered forward, lightning quick despite his bulk, and clasped a doughy hand around Zyra's neck.

'So fragile,' he wheezed, his triple chin waggling as he spoke. 'So very fragile.'

He began to squeeze.

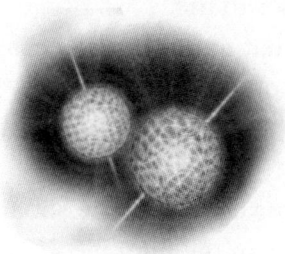

21: Ready to Devour

Tark and Tee emerged from the Forest, flanked by Gal and a group of armed Outers.

There were no VIs in the clearing. The static creature had assumed a vaguely human shape. It stood at the mouth of the cave, just inside the force-field, arms extended. Above each upturned palm floated a set of three squares. Little static pellets fired back and forth between the sets, as the squares dodged back and forth. One of the squares failed to dodge a pellet, and it disintegrated.

'Wot's it doin'?' whispered Tark.

'I have no idea,' Tee answered.

The figure closed its hands into fists, crushing the remaining squares.

'You can't win,' said the figure, its voice hollow and echoing.

'Says you.' Tark clutched his rapid-fire crossbow tighter.

'Every move you make. Every step you take.' A grim mirthless laughter filled the air around them.

'Brings you closer to me.'

'You know what to do?' said Tee, as he flicked the override switch on the IDD.

'Ya bets.' There was a grim determination in Tark's voice.

'Pawns moving across a chessboard.' There was more laughter from the figure.

'Force-field,' ordered Tee, taking aim.

Tark fumbled with the remote control device attached to his belt, dropped it, picked it up, and finally pressed the appropriate button. Gal rolled his eyes. The barrier shimmered out of existence and Tee fired.

Tee was barely able to hang on to the IDD as the discharge arced through the air to the creature. The energy crackled with a bright intensity that made Tark and the other Outers shield their eyes. The creature screeched and writhed, caught in the fiery, electric grasp. And then everything went silent.

For a moment, it was impossible to tell what had happened. The static was frozen within the almost-human shape, arms thrown back, head tilted crookedly. Then it began to pulsate – slowly at first, then faster. Growing, it took a lumbering step forward.

'I am ready,' it boomed. 'Ready to devour.'

'Move,' called Gal. Tee stepped aside as Gal and his team fired two rounds of static-tipped bolts. The creature laughed as the barrage melted into it.

'Tark!' Tee yelled, cradling the empty IDD in one hand, holding up the other.

Tark tossed the remote control to Tee, aimed his rapid-fire crossbow and pressed the trigger. A volley of bolts flew at the creature. It held up one misshaped hand and they ricocheted back towards the Outers. Tark continued to fire as Tee dropped to the ground and the Outers scattered. One of them cried out and hit the ground, a bolt in his leg.

'Stop!' yelled Tee.

A bolt slammed into the barrel of the rapid-fire crossbow, knocking it from Tark's hands.

The creature continued to grow, the static overflowing its human shape.

Tee hit the remote control and switched on the force-field.

A shimmer rippled through the air, catching the creature in its path. Sparks erupted and the creature howled; its growth halted.

'I doubt that's going to hold it for long,' said Tee, getting to his feet.

'Now wot?' asked Tark.

'We need to get back to base,' Tee answered. 'And prepare for an attack.'

He turned to Gal and the other Outers. The wounded man was being helped to his feet. 'You come back with me. The rest of you, stay here and keep an eye on that thing.' He met Gal's steely gaze. 'Do not engage it. And report any developments.'

'I'm staying,' announced Tark. Tee opened his mouth to protest, but Tark continued. 'There ain't nuthin' I can do ta 'elp ya prepare.'

Tee glanced at Gal.

'Yeah, I knows,' said Tark. 'He's in charge.'

'Stay safe.' Tee clapped him on the shoulder before heading off with the wounded Outer.

Tark picked up the rapid-fire crossbow, checked that it was still useable, and offered it to Gal. 'Don't has no effect on that thing in the cave. But if 'em VIs came backs.'

'You keep it,' said Gal.

***

Tark stood a few paces from the other Outers. They chatted amongst themselves in nervously hushed tones, but he silently stared at the creature. The air around it shimmered as it struggled against the force-field. His eyes were glued to the eddying static but his mind thought only of Zyra. Where was she? Was she safe? Would he ever see her again? He couldn't bear the thought of life without her.

'I luvs ya.' He mouthed the words quietly.

Laughter boomed from the creature, breaking into his thoughts.

'Devour!' it screamed and the force-field wavered. 'Devour everything!'

'That don't sound good,' said Tark.

Tark, Gal and the Outers watched in horrified fascination as a hole appeared in the shimmering air.

The creature poked a misshapen finger into the gap.

'It's breaking through,' shouted one of the Outers.

Static poured through the hole like a viscous liquid, pooling on the rocky ground. The creature within the force-field diminished as the pool grew.

'Shoot it!' Gal ordered.

'Tee said nots ta —' began Tark.

'Shoot it, or get out of the way,' said Gal, loading his crossbow. 'It's fighting against the force-field. And it's pushing its way out. It's probably weakened. This may be our last chance to stop it.'

Gal aimed his weapon and fired. The other Outers followed his lead.

The bolts had no effect and the river of grey continued to flow through the hole. Tark reluctantly aimed the rapid-fire crossbow.

'Give me that!' Gal snatched the weapon from Tark. 'If we can't stop it, you make sure to warn Tee.' He tossed his communicator to Tark.

Without waiting for a response, Gal strode forward and opened fire on the expanding pool of static. The bolts dissolved into its grey depths.

The creature behind the force-field shrank into nothingness as its substance escaped through the hole. The static on the ground undulated and surged forward, gurgling over Gal's booted feet.

Gal screamed. He saw his boots and leggings dispersing as the static rose to cover them. He forced himself to lift his eyes and continued firing.

'Stay back!' he called.

Tark hesitated.

One of the Outers, a young woman with short blonde hair, ignored Gal's order and dashed forward to help. Pulling off her cloak, she wrapped it around her hands and tried to wipe the static off Gal. The cloak stuck to it and moments later the woman's arms were covered in spreading greyness.

'Help!' she cried, struggling in vain. 'My arms! I can't feel my arms!'

'Run!' Gal yelled over his shoulder. The rapid-fire crossbow lost its solidity moments before the static rippled over it. 'Run!' The static rushed into Gal's mouth, drowning his words. Seconds later he and the woman were gone – consumed.

Tark retreated to the Forest, fumbling with the communicator, trying desperately to recover from what he had just seen.

'Comes on,' Tark called to the remaining Outers, who were still gaping at the roiling static. 'Gets back!' His voice snapped them out of their shocked inaction.

The Outers turned to run, but it was too late. A wave swelled across the expanding surface of the static and rushed at them. They wailed like panicked children as the wave crashed down. It engulfed them, wiping them away with frightening ease, and rolled on towards Tark.

Haunted faces seemed to loom up out of the

rushing swell, dead eyes fixed on Tark, their mouths wordlessly calling for him.

Tark ran. He stumbled over a tree root and crashed to the ground, the communicator flying off into the undergrowth. He picked himself up and struggled on for several minutes before allowing himself to glance back over his shoulder. What he saw made him stop and gape.

The creature was huge, and still growing. An amorphous blob of grey, a black maw in its centre. Images rippled across its surface. Faces, bodies, creatures – deformed and distorted. They extended from the conglomeration as if trying to escape, then snapped back to be swallowed into the swirling mass.

The static heaved across the landscape, consuming everything in its path. Animal life and vegetation disappeared into the expanding darkness at its centre. The only good thing about the feasting was that it slowed it down.

'Devour!' The word boomed through the Forest.

Tark ran. He did not look back. But the haunting sound of destruction followed him.

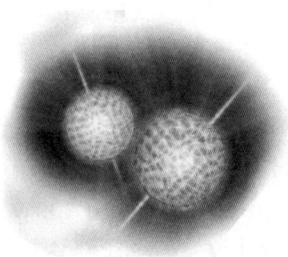

22: Bobby and the Fat Man

'Stop!' yelled Hope. 'Leave her alone.'

Hope grappled with the Fat Man, trying desperately to get him into a headlock. He knocked her aside as if he were swatting a fly.

'Bobby, no,' gasped Zyra, as she thrashed about, trying to escape his grip.

'It would be so easy to snap your pretty little neck,' wheezed the Fat Man, lifting her off the ground.

'Bobby, please.' Zyra's voice was now little more than a hoarse whisper. 'You're not him. You're Bobby. You're the Ultimate Gamer.'

'Talk about cheating,' screamed Hope, as she stumbled to her feet. 'You're not even playing now. You're just killing her.'

The Fat Man froze. His grip loosened a little and he looked into Zyra's green eyes, the whites spiked through with bloodshot rivulets.

'I've used so many different avatars that I sometimes forget who I really am.' He let go and Zyra dropped to the floor.

'I'm sorry.' Bobby stared down at Zyra, no trace of the Fat Man persona remaining. 'Each avatar has its own personality traits. Some are stronger than others, and the Fat Man is very strong.' His voice became almost a whisper. 'He doesn't like to lose, either.'

'Doesn't that bother you?' said Hope, helping Zyra to her feet.

'Nah,' said Bobby, all smiles again. 'Makes it more exciting.'

'You little snot-rag,' said Zyra, glaring at him and rubbing at her bruised throat. 'You're sick if you think this is exciting. We're not playing now and you could have killed me.'

'Everything's a game,' said Bobby. 'You guys trying to find me. Me tracking you down. You trying to get out of the environments and into the real world. Games. They're all games within games. Just without the Designers in control.'

'You think that trying to get out is a game?' asked Hope.

'Yeah. You want to get out, but you can't. I can get out, but I don't want to. I could let you out . . .' Bobby paused, looking at the eager expressions on their faces. 'But where's the fun in that? The only way I'll ever let you out, is if you play against me and win.' His eyes widened and he yelled, 'Without cheating!' His voice calmed instantly. 'Others have played against me, trying to win their way out. None of them succeeded.'

Bobby saw the look of surprise in Hope's eyes. 'No, you're not the first. It's not as if you're special or anything. There are non-gamers in other environments, you know. Hundreds of them. And they all want out. Sometimes a bunch of them will find a cheat code that mentions me. They come looking for me. I challenge them. We play. I win. They die.'

'Why, you little –' began Zyra.

'Don't.' Hope put a hand on her shoulder. 'He's trying to get you riled up. He wants you to do something stupid, like attack him or something. That would be a game to him.'

Bobby clasped his hands behind his back and feigned an innocent expression.

'You wouldn't be so smug if it was you in danger,' said Zyra.

'I'm always in danger,' said Bobby, suddenly serious. 'Being the Ultimate Gamer isn't about safety. I'm not part of the Designers' plan. I'm not wanted.'

'So, what have you got to be worried about?' asked Hope. 'What could possibly be a danger to you?'

As if on cue, two balls of static appeared over the top level of the pinball game.

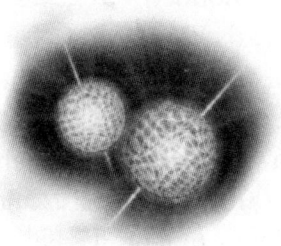

23: Preparations

The Outers' base was in a state of panic as Tark ran in. People were bustling about, shouting at each other and carrying equipment. Tee stood in the centre of it all, calling out instructions and answering frantic questions from passers-by.

'Yes,' he said to Chuck. 'Break out all the weapons. Arm as many people as you can.'

Tark weaved his way through the throng, making his way towards Tee as quickly as he could.

'What happened?' asked Tee.

'It gots out,' answered Tark.

'Where are the others? Where's Gal?'

Tark shook his head. 'It gots 'em. It's huge. It's . . . eatin' up everythin'. I thinks it's coming this way. We is done for.'

'Dear, dear, dear,' said the professor, scurrying up behind them. 'Are you sure it's going to attack us? I mean, it may have other plans, other intentions, other priorities. It may, it may.'

'I has gots no idea,' said Tark. 'But it ain't friendly.'

The professor nodded. 'Yes, yes, I see, yes.' He took a deep breath. 'Well, now, I have some other experimental weapons that we might be able to use.'

'What about the force-field?' asked Tee. 'It held it in the cave for a while. Can we somehow redirect the force-field from around our base and use it to hold the creature? Then maybe we could attack it with everything at once.'

'Hmm.' The professor scratched his head. 'Maybe, maybe, yes, maybe. I need to go have a sit down and think about it.'

'Sits down?' sputtered Tark. 'Ya betta makes it quick!'

Tee's communicator beeped and he lifted it to his ear.

'Rylan here,' came a voice, broken up by hissing and crackling. 'I've reached the top of the cliff. I can see . . .' His words were swallowed up by interference.

'I'm losing you,' called Tee.

'It's massive.' Rylan's voice was back. 'It's tearing through the Forest. Swallowing it up!' And then it was gone again.

'Rylan!' shouted Tee. 'Can you hear me? Is it headed for the base?'

Rylan's muffled voice was barely audible, now. 'We don't stand a chance.' The connection went dead.

Then it sprang back to life with a new voice, rumbling like oncoming thunder. 'Devour!'

Tee's expression was grave as he snapped the

communicator shut and looked at the professor. 'We need everything you've got and we need it fast.'

The professor shuddered. 'Oh dear, oh dear, oh dear. Why is it coming here? It shouldn't be coming here. That's not good. Not at all. At all.'

'Listen up, everyone.' Tee climbed up onto a couple of storage crates as the Outers gathered around him.

'We're in for a hell of a fight.' He paused. 'And, in all honesty, I don't know that we can win it.' He paused again, choosing his words carefully. 'But we have to try. Not just for ourselves, but for all future Outers. Because if there is one certainty in this contrived, artificial, imposed world – it is that there will always be more of us. There will be other characters, other versions of ourselves –' he looked directly at Tark '– who will stand up and say *No*. So for the sake of all these future Outers, as well as for ourselves, we now come to the point where we must again say *No*. We will not lie down and die. We will fight for our existence. We will fight for our freedom.'

A cheer went up from the Outers.

'Win or lose,' continued Tee, his eyes moving about the common room, meeting gaze after gaze. 'Whatever the outcome, we will achieve it without the Designers. Win or lose, we are free!'

As another cheer made its way through the crowd, Professor Palimpsest clasped his hands together. 'Free,' he whispered. 'Are we really?'

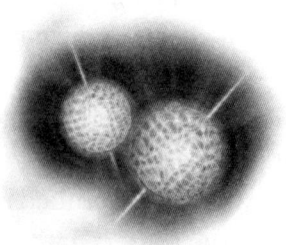

24: Antibodies

'Time to play,' announced Bobby, whirling around and transforming into the Pinball Wizard. 'This time, you two can come with me and watch.'

He waved his wand above him and a dome of glass enclosed the entire game. Waving it again, he rose into the air, Zyra and Hope rising with him.

The VIs charged them.

'Watch out!' called Hope as the three of them sped towards the glass. Upon reaching it, they simply passed through, finally coming to a stop high above the pinball game. The VIs streaked towards them, but they collided with the glass, writhing angrily, trapped in the game.

'Sudden Death Aerial Pinball,' the Pinball Wizard called out at the top of his voice. He waved his wand yet again.

Five silver balls spat from the mouth of the plastic clown and careened around the bottom level of the game. As the first ball bumped into a rubber ring, it bounced off and up into the air – straight for the closest VI. It collided and exploded in a shower of sparks, destroying its target.

'Yes!' The Pinball Wizard punched the air above him. The propeller on his tall hat spun excitedly. The other four balls were launched at the second VI, which zoomed off to the back of the game.

The VI was trapped, four silver balls converging on it from different directions. They hit simultaneously. The explosion was huge, bursting apart the over-sized pinball machine in a blinding flash, shattering the glass casing. Zyra and Hope raised their arms to shield their faces.

As quiet descended, they opened their eyes and lowered their arms. They were standing in an endless meadow of golden flowers, a crystal-clear, blue-as-blue-can-be sky above, with Bobby standing smugly beside them.

'Had to move us,' he explained. 'There were bound to be more antibodies.'

'What?' asked Hope.

'You're not very bright, are you?' Bobby said. 'The balls of sparkly static. They're not nice. They're out to get me. Sooo . . . I moved us to a different environment. Now they have to start looking all over again. They're easy enough to fight if there's only a couple of them. But they always call for help.' He picked a flower and held it out to Hope. 'And I thought you might like this place. I do. Good place to rest.'

'I get it,' said Hope, ignoring the offer. 'But what did you call them?'

'Antibodies,' said Bobby, tossing the flower over his shoulder.

'You mean those things aren't viruses?' There was a distinct, desperate edge to Hope's voice.

'Viruses?' Bobby burst into gales of laughter. 'Viruses!' He clutched his stomach and bent double, falling amongst the flowers.

'Would someone let us in on the joke?' said Zyra, hands on hips, glaring at Bobby. 'Just what is so funny?'

'They're not viruses,' spluttered Bobby, his head popping up above the sea of blooms. His laughter subsided. He looked from Zyra's confused face to Hope's worried expression. 'You have no idea, do you?'

'No idea about what?' asked Zyra tersely.

'I'm beginning to get it,' said Hope slowly.

'I'm the virus,' said Bobby, beaming with pride. 'I'm the one who doesn't follow the rules. Heck, I make my own rules. I'm the one they're trying to delete.'

'They've been after us, too,' said Zyra.

'Well, yes,' said Bobby. 'Of course they have. You're a corrupted file. You've chosen not to play. And as for her.' He shifted his gaze to Hope. 'Well, she's the offspring of two corrupted files. Which, I guess, sort of makes her a virus too.' He paused, then added, 'But I'm a much more important virus. I cause a lot more disruption. It's me they're really after.'

'Oh, no.' Hope's legs gave out under her and she sat down hard, disappearing into the flowers.

'Oh, come on,' said Bobby. 'It's not that big a deal. They've been chasing me for . . . forever.'

'No, it's not that.' Hope shook her head slowly and placed it in her hands. 'It's the weapon.'

'What weapon?' asked Bobby and Zyra together.

'Professor Palimpsest has been developing a new weapon,' explained Hope.

'Palimpsest?' A worried look crossed Bobby's face.

'He's been working on a way of harnessing the substance of the Interface into a weapon. It's all based on the theory that the VIs and the other static creature in the cave are viruses. My father was banking on this weapon giving us the advantage.'

'What creature?' asked Bobby, his face stony.

'There's this thing in a cave in our environment,' explained Hope. 'It's much larger that the VIs. We thought it was a virus and that it might be controlling the VIs. Father had a force-field put around it to keep it there until we had something that could deal with it.'

'No.' Bobby shook his head gravely. 'It's the antivirus program and it controls the antibodies. It's the brains of the operation and this is its standard MO – it hides, usually at the edge of some environment, where there are weak spots.'

'Like the alcove in the common room, with the static,' said Zyra, remembering her introduction to the Outers' base.

'It needs slow access to the Interface in order to strengthen and grow,' explained Bobby. 'Too much, and it could get overwhelmed. So it hides while it slowly charges up, until it's ready to make an attempt at wiping me off the face of the game.'

'How do you know so much about this antivirus program?' asked Zyra.

'We've met before.' One corner of Bobby's mouth curled up into an odd half-smile. 'It almost got me. But I beat it. Chased it away. It couldn't deal with my games. It couldn't understand any game other than the Designers' game.' His expression became thoughtful. 'It must have been rebuilding itself. Getting stronger. Making a plan. And you Outers must be part of that plan.'

Bobby paced up and down through the flowers, crushing them under his feet. 'Palimpsest. An Interface weapon. Antibodies eating up corrupted files. Deleting them. And now it's almost ready. Ready to get me. And if you use this weapon against it, you'll make it stronger.'

'What if the weapon has enough of the Interface to overwhelm it?' Hope clutched at the idea as if it were a raft in a raging sea.

Bobby shook his head. 'Not unless it has a

continuous connection to the Interface. And I'm betting it doesn't.'

'So, what do we do?' asked Zyra.

'There's only one thing to do.' Bobby stopped pacing. He looked steadily at Zyra and slowly shifted his gaze to Hope.

'Time to play – for real!'

Bobby threw his arms up and everything around them burst into colour.

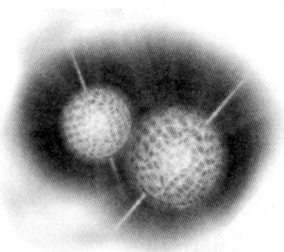

25: The Ultimate Gamer

Blinded by an explosion of colour, everyone in the common room stopped what they had been doing. As normality returned they saw that a golden podium had appeared in the centre of the cavern. Standing on either side, looking as dazed as everyone else in the room, were Zyra and Hope.

Tark immediately ran to Zyra, throwing his arms around her, hugging her tightly. Tee ran to Hope, enclosing her in a protective embrace.

'Touching reunion,' said a voice from atop the podium. 'But really, we do not have time.'

Everyone looked up. Three rotating loops of gold spun around a suspended black chair in which sat a figure of silver. Thin, shiny and human in shape, with a vaguely masculine form, he looked like he was made of liquid metal, constantly moving within an invisible mould – one perfect, seamless whole. He raised an arm with a fluid motion that was too perfect.

'Correct me if I am wrong, but we are soon to be

under attack.' He had no facial features, even when he spoke. His androgynous voice seemed to emanate from him.

'Is that . . .' began Tark.

'The Ultimate Gamer?' asked Tee.

Zyra gasped. 'Bobby?'

'I am the Ultimate Gamer,' said the figure without a mouth. 'I am the ability to play, personified. I am instinct and reflex and speed. I am strength and intelligence. I am your only hope against the antivirus program.'

'Antivirus program?' said Tee. 'What's it talking about?'

'That thing in the cave,' explained Hope. 'It's an antivirus program. It's been designed to find and delete any virus programs or corrupted files.'

Tee's eyes widened.

'Yeah,' said Hope. 'To it, we are the corrupted files that need to be destroyed.'

'I thoughts it wuz a virus,' said Tark. 'At least, that's wot he says.' Tark pointed to Professor Palimpsest.

'Of course he said it was a virus,' said the Ultimate Gamer.

'Wot does that mean?' demanded Tark.

'What *does* that mean?' asked Tee, turning to look at Palimpsest.

'Ah, well, well, well,' said the professor, fumbling with the buttons on his lab coat, and looking from one expectant face to another. 'That's what it told me to say. Yes, yes. Yes.'

For a moment there was silence.

'Ya is a traitor?' Tark blurted out.

'No, no, no.' Palimpsest shook his head vigorously. 'Most definitely no, no, no. It said that it would not harm the Outers if I did what it asked. Yes. It said that it was only interested in the Ultimate Gamer. Yes. It said that it would leave us in peace if I found some way for it to tap into the power of the Interface more quickly, without danger of overload. Yes. Because it needed that power to defeat the Ultimate Gamer. Yes, yes.'

'The IDD,' said Tark. 'We wuz givin' it power.'

The professor nodded his head apologetically. 'I am afraid so. Yes. Yes. But it was necessary. Now that the Ultimate Gamer has been found, all we need to do is hand him over. Yes. Then it, and the antibodies, will leave us alone.'

'That will not solve the situation,' said the Ultimate Gamer. 'It is an antivirus program. It is designed to wipe anything that deviates from the will of the Designers. You deviate, as do I. As far as it is concerned, we are one and the same.'

'No, no, no,' said the professor. 'That cannot be right. No.'

A young man came running into the common room, panic in his eyes. 'That static thing is only a few minutes away,' he said, between panting breaths.

'Tell everyone to fall back,' ordered Tee.

'Oh,' said the professor. 'Perhaps I was wrong to believe it? Yes, yes, perhaps.'

'He could not help it,' announced the Ultimate Gamer. 'It is in his programming. His base coding is easily overwritten, making him particularly susceptible to outside influences.'

'What, what, what?' The professor took his glasses off and ran a hand over his eyes and brow. His voice dropped to a whisper. 'No.'

'So how is we gonna fights this thing?' asked Tark.

'I will play against the antivirus program,' said the Ultimate Gamer.

An image appeared, hovering like a large view screen in front of the podium. It showed the area outside the base. In the distance, they could see the spark and fizzle of the approaching antivirus program as it tore through the Forest like a tornado of static.

'What makes you think that you are capable of beating the program?' asked the professor. 'Hmmm?'

'I may not be capable,' said the silver figure. 'But we have crossed paths before. And since then, I have been preparing. As, no doubt, it has been.'

'Are you sure this thing's an antivirus program?' asked Tee, still staring at the destruction on the screen. 'It seems to be behaving more like a virus. It's not just wiping corrupted files. It's consuming everything.'

'It is different from the last time,' admitted the gamer. 'But it still needs to be fought.' He stretched his hands out in front of him. 'Engage games mode.'

Numerous holographic keyboards appeared before

him within the rotating loops. They surrounded him like a multi-levelled, techno church organ. As his hands flew over the keys, a three-dimensional grid made of green light took shape on the screen. Crisscrossing emerald beams filled up almost the entire area between the base entrance and the start of the Forest.

Pixels of intense white light appeared within the grid, one by one, taking on a human outline. As each pinpoint of light solidified, a new one would appear, filling in more details, and soon the shape had substance. Encased in shiny silver armour, with a sword o'light in one hand and a shield in the other, stood a knight.

A holographic joystick, with a multitude of buttons across its body, materialised in front of the Ultimate Gamer. He reached out a silver hand and wrapped it around the insubstantial gaming control as if it were really there. The liquid silver of its hand seemed to meld with the hologram, becoming part of it. As the gamer's hand moved the joystick, the knight on the screen raised its sword and cut a figure eight path through the air.

'Sixty seconds to engagement,' said the gamer.

'Everyone out of here!' shouted Tee. 'Get as far back into the caves as you can.'

There was a rush of people towards the storage area that extended deep into the mountainside.

Tark, Zyra and Hope stood their ground.

'You too,' said Tee.

'Not a chance!' answered Zyra.

The professor scurried towards Research.

'Not you,' called Tee. 'This is all your fault. You're staying.'

The professor hung his head and shuffled back.

Tee flipped open his communicator and glanced up at the screen. At the edge of the image he could see a small group of armed Outers lying in wait by the boulders near the entrance. 'Get inside,' he ordered.

There was no response. He tried again, flicking it on and off.

'Devour!' The voice boomed from the communicator.

'Damn!' Tee flung the device across the room. It snapped apart when it hit the ground.

Zyra looked from the screen to the gamer, back to the screen and back to the gamer again, as the antivirus program moved closer.

'Are you Bobby's avatar?' she asked. 'Or was he yours?'

The figure glanced down at her. 'Does it matter?'

On the screen, the edge of the Forest disappeared and the antivirus program was finally revealed – an amorphous mass with a huge, gaping black hole in its centre.

'Let's play!' At that moment, the silver figure sounded almost like Bobby.

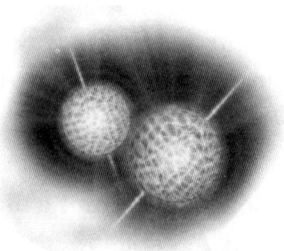

26: Battle in the Light Grid – Chimaera vs Knight

The antivirus program ravenously careened into the light grid, mouth wide open, ready to consume. It touched the edge of the trap and, in a rush of static, was sucked into the grid, condensed to less than half its previous size. It screeched and howled as a multitude of manic faces momentarily rippled across its surface. It whirled like a tornado, throwing itself against the sides of the grid. Green energy crackled at every touch, coursing through the program and making it scream louder.

Finally the program ceased its struggles. It settled onto the ground into a nebulous mass.

'You want to play?' A deep, gurgling sound emerged from the creature. 'I have been learning to play.'

The creature undulated and pulsed. A lion's head grew from its depths, roaring as it emerged. The static continued to take shape – a lion's body formed, with muscular legs and sharp, sharp claws. From its rear, in place of a tail, snaked a serpent with wild eyes and long fangs, hissing and spitting as it thrashed about. From the middle of the lion's back sprang the head of a goat, with fierce eyes of fire, twisted horns and snapping jaws. It was an impossible creature, three animals in one, with an ungainly appearance.

The chimaera's three heads gnashed their static teeth, sparking and sizzling, the creature's bulk dwarfing the knight. It crouched low to the ground, its serpent tail flicking from one side to the other, forked tongue darting in and out of its mouth. It crept towards the knight as if stalking prey, then paused. Fixing three sets of eyes on its opponent, it leapt.

The knight flung itself to one side, swinging the sword o'light. As the chimaera leapt past, the sword came down on its tail, severing the serpent from the rest of the creature. The decapitated snake shrieked and spat, writhing on the ground, before dissolving into nothingness.

The chimaera howled with its two remaining heads and launched itself at the knight, the lion's jaws ready to savage its prey.

The knight sprang forward, faster than anything wearing armour had a right to. It thrust upwards with its weapon.

The sword o'light sliced into the belly of the beast as it sailed over the head of the knight. The static that made up its form parted like the Red Sea and landed in a shapeless heap.

A cheer went up from the few Outers who had remained at the entrance of the base. Emboldened, they crept closer to the grid.

The knight barely had time to turn around before the static took on a new shape. Within seconds a huge dragon, larger even than the chimaera, was glaring down at the knight. It threw back its head and roared a deep and guttural sound with a crackly, electronic undertone.

'Plaaay!'

The dragon reared on its hind legs and thrust its head forward, jaws wide open. A burst of orange flame erupted from its mouth.

The knight held up its shield, deflecting the flames.

Back on all fours, the dragon roared again. It lifted an enormous, lumbering foot, ready to charge its opponent.

The knight sprang forward with the same movement it had used against the chimaera, thrusting upwards with the sword. Although the sword o'light sliced up into the gigantic foot, it was not enough to stop it. The dragon's foot stomped to the ground, crushing the knight beneath it.

A booming voice roared through the grid. 'I have been learning to win!'

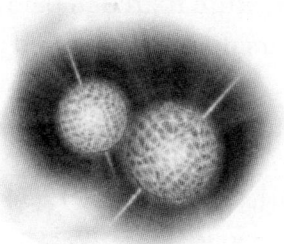

27: Charging Up

The Ultimate Gamer let go of the joystick. His sheen had faded and his colour darkened with patches of grey and black.

'Are you okay?' called Zyra.

'No,' answered the Ultimate Gamer. 'The antivirus program is stronger than I had anticipated.'

'The IDD,' said Tark, glaring at the professor.

The professor cringed, but as Tark looked away, his face brightened. 'Of course! Yes, yes, yes. That is it!'

'It is more than that,' said the Ultimate Gamer. 'It *is* different from the last time I encountered it. It has learned to play. It is . . . enjoying the game.'

Unnoticed, the professor edged his way across the common room and slipped out towards his workshop.

On the screen, the dragon was grinding its foot into the ground. It swung its body around and lumbered across the light grid, throwing its bulk against the perimeter. The grid crackled with energy, snaking tendrils of green coursing through the dragon.

Although the creature roared in pain, it continued to push. The Outers that had gathered around the grid shrank back.

The Ultimate Gamer took hold of the joystick. 'Resume play.'

Looking up at the screen, Zyra and the others saw pinpricks of light forming into a new shape – a dragon, albeit a smaller one. The larger dragon stepped back from the grid perimeter and charged its new opponent.

As the dragons on the screen reared up and grappled with each other, claws slashing, mouths spewing fire, Professor Palimpsest came rushing back into the common room, the newly charged IDD clutched in his arms.

'This is it. This is it. This is it!' He scurried towards the Ultimate Gamer's podium.

'Stop him!' shouted Tee.

Tark and Zyra ran at the professor. As Tark wrestled the IDD from his hands, Zyra pinned the professor's arms behind his back.

'No, no, no,' the professor cried. 'I'm trying to help! Yes!'

Zyra gave his arm a twist, making him yelp.

'Yeah, sure ya is,' said Tark, levelling the IDD at the professor's chest. 'Wonder wots would 'appen if I gaves ya a burst o' this?'

The professor shook his head frantically.

An agonised wail brought their attention back to

the screen. The Ultimate Gamer's dragon was on the ground. The larger dragon ripped it apart with its claws, literally wrenching off one of its arms.

Hope looked away from the screen, sickened. 'There must be something we can do to help!'

With a shudder, the Ultimate Gamer released the joystick and slumped back in his chair. Growing patches of black spread through his body like oil spills.

'I can help!' yelled the professor.

Zyra tightened her grip on his arms.

'The IDD gave the power of the Interface to the antivirus program. Yes.' The professor struggled against his captor as he spoke. 'The Ultimate Gamer could, perhaps, also tap into this power.'

'Possibly.' The gamer lifted a feeble hand and tapped a key. A panel slid back on the side of the podium. 'Connect it.'

The professor tried to get free, but Zyra held him fast. 'Please, please, please. You've got –'

A piercing scream cut the professor off.

On the screen, the static dragon was pressed up against the grid's perimeter. One of its clawed feet had broken through and was clutching the leg of an Outer, dragging him towards the grid. Several Outers held onto his arms, pulling, trying to save him.

'That's Chuck.' Zyra's voice was barely a whisper.

'Let him go,' called Tee, pointing at the professor.

Palimpsest grabbed the IDD from Tark and

scurried to the podium. He examined it quickly then stuck the end of the device into a connection port. 'Hope, hope, hope,' he said, squeezing the trigger.

The Ultimate Gamer sat bolt upright as static zipped around the gold loops that encircled him.

On the screen, the dragon had won the deadly tug-o-war. It yanked Chuck into the grid, bellowed a victory roar, and snapped its jaws on him. Chuck exploded in a burst of dissipating pixels. The dragon then thrust its claws back through the grid's perimeter.

The Ultimate Gamer's hand shot forward and grasped the joystick. 'I'm back,' he said, in Bobby's voice. 'And I'm charged.'

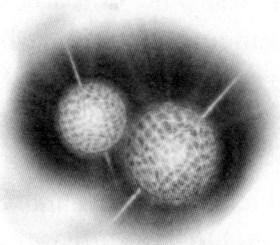

28: Battle in the Light Grid – Dragon vs Unicorn

The dismembered dragon dispersed into pinpoints of light, as if its very molecules had separated. Like a cloud of fireflies they swarmed through the grid and gathered around the head of the larger dragon. The creature roared, snapping at the lights and bringing its foot back into the grid. As the perimeter repaired itself, the dots of light left the dragon, swarmed to the other end of the grid and took form.

The dragon looked down at the unicorn. It paused, assessing its new opponent, then reared up. Thrusting its head forward, it opened its jaws wide and flames spewed forth.

The unicorn backed away as the flames hit the ground where it had stood. It pawed at the ground and bucked, shaking its head from side to side, its sparkly white mane and forelock fluttering majestically.

'Oh, yes.' The dragon spoke in guttural tones, barely distinguishable from a roar. 'Bring it on!'

Again, the dragon reared back and released an

onslaught of flames. The unicorn dodged to one side with a movement that seemed both impossible and extremely un-equine. It steadied itself, planting all fours firmly, looking up at its opponent with crystal-clear, ice-blue eyes. It bent its right front leg and lowered its head, as if kneeling. Still on its hind legs, the dragon laughed and roared in triumph as it charged.

But the unicorn was not submitting. Its spiralling horn glowed with a pearlescence that began at the base and extended to the point. The dragon ceased its roar as a blaze of light surged from the unicorn's horn. The light encompassed the dragon. It lashed out with its claws, but to no effect. The light had substance, and it constricted the creature's movement. The dragon's forelegs were pushed in against its body. Its head began to bear down – the neck squashing into the torso. The light formed into a sphere, forcing the static to lose the dragon shape completely. The light sphere got smaller and smaller, compressing the static.

The static spun within the sphere of light, around and around with giddying speed, like a whirlpool. The sphere wavered, bending towards the whirling mass. With increasing speed, it was sucked into the depths of the static, like galaxies into a black hole.

The spinning ball undulated, its surface like a stormy sea, anguished faces occasionally bobbing to the surface. Expanding, it began to morph again.

Not waiting to see what form it would take, the unicorn pawed at the ground like an enraged bull and attacked the static. Its glowing horn plunged into the depths of its adversary. As the unicorn tried to back up for another assault, it found that it could not retract its horn, no matter how hard it pulled.

The enlarging mass of static rose up into the air, taking the unicorn with it, legs flailing helplessly.

Shooting up to the top of the light grid in a sudden, violent motion, the static rammed the unicorn into the edge of the grid. Green sparks engulfed the animal, crackles of energy coursing over the white surface of its body. As the static lowered a little, the light abated and the unicorn went limp, its mane singed, its hooves smouldering. The now dull horn cracked and split apart at the base, as the unicorn's body fell.

The moment it hit the ground, it fragmented into myriad pinpoints of light.

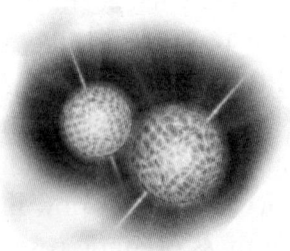

29: Super-charged

'It hasn't been wiping files and programs,' gasped the Ultimate Gamer as he released the joystick. 'It's been absorbing them. Every virus program, every corrupt file has become a part of it.'

'What does that mean?' asked Zyra.

'It has become a virus itself. The ultimate virus. Ready to consume . . . everything.'

'You have the power of the Interface,' said the professor. 'Yes. You do. You can defeat it. Yes. You can.'

The Ultimate Gamer held up his hands in front of his featureless face, turning them one way and then the other. 'It is not enough. The program will win.'

'More, more, more,' said the professor excitedly. 'We can give you more. Yes.' He paced up and down. 'I can charge up the IDD again and again. Yes. Or?' He stopped pacing. 'Or a direct link up to the Interface.'

'That may work,' said the Ultimate Gamer. 'But time will be limited.'

The professor rushed off to his workshop.

'What do you mean by "time will be limited"?' asked Zyra.

'The raw power of the Interface, in a constant feed, will be impossible to contain,' explained the Ultimate Gamer. 'It will give me power. But it will eventually overwhelm me.'

'How much time will you have?' asked Hope.

'I don't know.' It was Bobby's voice and it was barely a whisper.

On the screen the antivirus program had taken on the form of a robot. All sharp jutting angles and lethal weaponry, it was an arsenal on squat, boxy legs. It was blasting away at the grid perimeter with various guns protruding from its mechanical arms.

The professor came back into the common room dragging the end of a cable. 'This is a link to the Interface via my switchboard.' He plugged the cable into the connection port on the podium. 'The cable carries a greater amount of charge per second than you can possibly use. More than enough to destroy you instantly. You will need to monitor and control the amount you take in.'

The Ultimate Gamer inclined his head stiffly.

'Good.' The professor pointed back over this shoulder. 'I need to go and switch it on. Yes.' He rushed back out again.

On the screen, a hole had appeared in the perimeter. The robot blasted away at it.

'I'm scared.' It was Bobby's voice.

The power of the Interface charged along the cable to the podium.

The Ultimate Gamer arched his back as the power thundered through him, his silvery lustre returned tenfold. The loops around him sparked with energy as they increased in speed. The holographic keyboards and joystick disappeared as he stood, spreading his arms. His hands extended towards the loops, which spun so fast it looked as if he were enclosed in a sphere of static. When his silvery fingertips skimmed the spinning loops, he became a ball of blistering brilliance.

There was a collective intake of breath from the audience. The professor squinted through his glasses as he scurried back into the common room.

On screen the light grid changed from green to static grey. The breach sealed itself, the impact of the robot's continual blasting now having no effect. The pinpoints of light unified, taking on a familiar bulky shape.

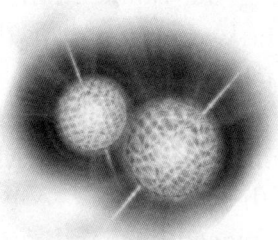

30: Battle in the Light Grid – Static Man vs Fat Man

The Fat Man was carrying a bazooka. He aimed and fired three shots. The first shattered the robot's arm. The second knocked the robot to the ground. The third blew apart its head. The static of the antivirus program collapsed into a formless heap.

The Fat Man tossed aside the empty weapon and strode across the grid. By the time he reached the antivirus program, it was already taking a human shape, mirroring its adversary. The Static Man was the same height and breadth as the Fat Man, but instead of fat, its bulk was made of muscle. Pulling an arm back, it threw a punch at the Fat Man. The static fist connected with the Fat Man's jaw, sending him sprawling.

The Static Man chuckled as it loomed over its opponent. 'I know what you've done. It won't help. The Interface will consume you from the inside out while I watch.'

The Fat Man spun on the ground, scissoring his

legs and knocking the Static Man to the ground. Within seconds he was on top of it, throwing punch after punch. Each time he hit the static face, its features rippled and changed momentarily, different faces superimposing onto the Static Man's body. The faces laughed with every blow.

The Fat Man placed his hands around the Static Man's throat, squeezing with all his might. The Static Man reached up and did the same, shifting its weight. The battling opponents tumbled across the ground from one end of the grid to the other.

They hit the perimeter, energy arcing through them, forcing them apart. The Fat Man got to his feet first, but the Static Man kicked out, connecting with its opponent's substantial gut. The Fat Man was propelled into the air. He slammed into the grid perimeter. Energy crackled and sparked as he fell to the ground.

The Static Man casually got to its feet and sauntered across the grid. 'Once I have defeated you, I will consume the Outers, savouring each and every byte of each and every corrupted file.' His voice was an ominous, hollow rumble. 'I will pick apart the bones of their binary coding and assimilate their strengths. And then . . .' It sneered. 'And then, nothing will stand in my way. I will make my way across Designers Paradise, devour every environment, eating every program, every file, every skerrick of data. I will amalgamate everything within my coding and I shall become the one and only program.'

'Sounds familiar,' breathed the Fat Man, struggling to his feet. 'But to what purpose? You are an antivirus program.'

'Don't you see? Everything is corrupt. Everything must be cleansed. Only when all things are me, can I ensure that no viruses shall come into being.'

'You're wrong,' said the Fat Man. 'There will still be a virus.'

The Static Man tilted its head.

'The worst possible virus – you!' The Fat Man murmured an incantation under his breath. The earth beneath the Static Man moved around its feet. The Static Man was unable to take a step as the ground itself rose up around its ankles. It crept up, forming a mound as it reached past the static knees.

'Anything you can do, I can do better,' sang the Static Man. It invoked a spell and the ground beneath the Fat Man encased his own feet and began to rise.

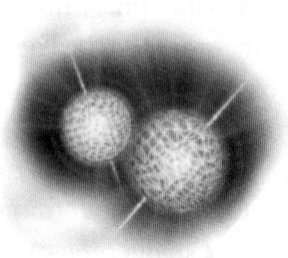

31: Plans

As the battle progressed on screen, Tark noticed Professor Palimpsest edging out of the common room again. Tark was certain that something wasn't right. Everyone else's attention was focussed on the screen, so he easily slipped away and followed the professor to his workshop.

Tark peered in. The professor's back was turned while he fumbled intently with something on the main workbench. His instincts had been correct; the professor was up to something.

'Wot ya doin'?' demanded Tark, entering the workshop.

The professor jumped and whirled around. His left sleeve was rolled up, a rough tourniquet above the elbow. In his right hand he held a syringe filled with the static of the Interface, a long needle at its end.

'Preparing to make amends,' said the professor, gravely.

'Wot?' asked Tark.

'The Ultimate Gamer has a limited time in which to defeat the antivirus program, before the Interface consumes him from within.' The professor spoke steadily, all trace of his eccentric programmed speech pattern gone – suppressed by a new determination. 'He will not win without some help. This is my fault, so I shall provide that help. I need to distract the program. Find a weakness, perhaps.'

'And how does ya plan on doing that?'

'Like this.' The professor jabbed the needle into a vein on his arm, and injected the static. 'Now I will enter the grid and let the antivirus program consume me. The static patches prevented the antibodies from finding us, and so I am hoping that enough of it coursing through my bloodstream will shield my coding once I have been assimilated.'

'But ya'll die.'

'I will die anyway.'

'We is all gonna die if we don't defeats the program,' said Tark. 'With yar help we mights be able ta come up with anotha plan.'

'You misunderstand me. I will die no matter what. The dose I have just injected will soon kill me.' He tossed the syringe onto the workbench. 'So get out of my way. The sooner I am assimilated by the antivirus program, the more time I will have to make a difference.'

The professor walked past Tark.

'Waits,' called Tark. 'There's gotta be sumthin'

else the rest of us can do.' He looked around the workshop and spotted the empty IDD. 'Wot about that thing?'

'No,' said the professor, stopping at the door. 'No. It does not hold enough charge. You would simply be giving the antivirus program more power.'

'But –' Tark's voice was tinged with desperation.

'Matters are out of your hands.' The professor headed out the door mumbling, 'Out, out, out.'

Tark lowered his eyes and saw the cable snaking its way to the alcove at the back of the workshop, a soft sizzling glow emanating from the darkness. His eyes followed the cable up to the professor's switchbox. 'I wunda.'

He rummaged through the professor's workshop, looking in the piles of equipment on the workbenches, the boxes full of spare parts and the lockers with additional equipment. Finally he found what he needed under the main workbench.

Tark made his way back to the common room and sidled up to Zyra.

'I has an idea,' he whispered.

'Shhh,' Zyra responded. 'Look.' She pointed up at the screen.

The Fat Man and the Static Man were still exchanging blows. The Fat Man's clothes were ragged and he was bleeding from wounds on his face. His steps were faltering, his punches often mistimed and having little effect. By contrast the Static Man was full of energy, leaping about and delivering well-placed blows that sent its opponent staggering and falling.

Tark looked over at the Ultimate Gamer. He had again lost his sheen, with a spreading blackness inking its way through the liquid silver.

Tark shook Zyra's shoulder urgently. 'I've gots an idea and I needs yar 'elp.'

'What?' asked Zyra, looking away from the screen.

'Ya needs ta come with me ta the professor's workshop,' said Tark. 'I thinks there's a way we can 'elps the gamer dude.'

Tee and Hope gasped, eyes glued to the screen. Tark and Zyra looked up.

Professor Palimpsest was reaching out a hand to the light grid. He touched the perimeter and was suddenly inside. He strode across the grid to where the Static Man stood over the slumped form of the Fat Man.

'Excuse me,' he said. 'This really is not acceptable behaviour. No. No. No.'

The Static Man turned around and grabbed the professor in a big bear-hug. Palimpsest slowly sank into the static, his features distorting and dispersing until there was nothing left of him.

Hope gasped again and Tee muttered, 'What was he trying to prove?'.

'Now,' hissed Tark. 'We've gots ta go now.'

'All right,' said Zyra, as Tark led her out of the

common room and into the workshop. 'What's this brilliant idea of yours?'

'What's this brilliant idea of yours?' repeated Tark. He paused and looked suspiciously at Zyra. 'Wot's with the fancy talk?'

'Oh.' Zyra waved her hand dismissively. 'I've decided to overcome my programming.'

'Why?' he demanded.

'Because it's what I want to do.' Zyra put her hands on her hips and narrowed her eyes, daring Tark to make an issue of it. 'Now tell me about your idea.'

Tark stared at her for a moment before answering. 'We needs ta overload the antivirus program.' He patted the IDD on the workbench.

'That won't work,' said Zyra. 'We need a direct feed to the Interface in order to overload it.'

'We will,' said Tark, picking up a roll of cable. 'We plugs one end inta the IDD and the other inta one of 'em cracks in the wall.'

Zyra played with the stud in her lip and swiped at her hair. 'What if it overloads the IDD?'

Tark shrugged. 'At leasts we'll have tried.'

'Okay,' said Zyra. 'You better have a long lead.'

Tark passed the cable to Zyra. 'This 'ere is the longest I could finds.'

Zyra examined it. 'This won't go very far. We need to find an exposed area of Interface closer to the cave entrance.'

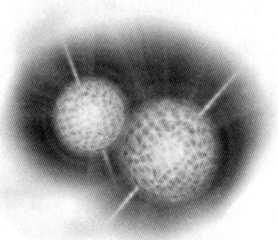

32: Battle in the Light Grid – Endgame

The Static Man turned its attention back to the Fat Man, who was standing again. 'Time to end this, I think.'

'No,' said Professor Palimpsest.

'What?' The Static Man looked around for the disembodied voice.

'What's the matter?' grunted the Fat Man as he threw a punch, hitting the Static Man in the gut.

The Static Man doubled over and the Fat Man kneed it in the face, sending it staggering back. The Static Man quickly recovered its balance, taking a menacing step forward.

As the Fat Man watched, a face rippled across the surface of the Static Man's stomach.

'Indigestion?' asked the Fat Man. 'You should be careful what you eat.'

'I can control this,' said the Static Man.

The Fat Man hit it in the face. 'Really?' He hit it again. 'You sure?' And again.

The Static Man fell over, a face bubbling up in its chest.

'There's only one way to defeat it,' said Professor Palimpsest's face. 'One, one, one. Interface. Unleashed. Full force. Will overload it.'

'But –' the Fat Man began but the professor cut him off.

'Yes, yes, I know. It will kill, kill, kill you as well.' The professor's face wavered momentarily. 'It's the only way. Only way.' The face contorted. 'Ahhh.' The professor's face separated as if being pulled apart by unseen hands, dissolving back into the static.

The Static Man sat up. 'I have dismembered his coding.' The Static Man stood. 'And now I shall dismember yours.'

'I *will* defeat you,' chuckled the Fat Man.

The Fat Man clasped his hands together, forming a double fist, and thrust it at the Static Man. A rush of static poured from the Fat Man's hands, ramming into the Static Man, forcing it back against the grid's perimeter. The Static Man howled with rage as it thrashed and twisted under the continual impact.

'You'll destroy yourself,' yelled the Static Man.

'And take you with me,' said the Fat Man.

With great effort the Fat Man closed in step-by-step, power rushing through him and into his opponent. The Static Man lost its form, its face becoming blobby and misshapen, its arms melting into its sides.

As he neared, the Fat Man's steps began to falter. The Static Man reformed. 'It's doing more damage to you than me. I'm stronger. I can survive longer than you. You can't channel enough.'

The Fat Man staggered to his knees, still discharging the Interface into the Static Man. But the discharge was weakening.

'It's frying your coding.' The Static Man took a step forward, pushing against the discharge of energy. 'You are channelling less and less.'

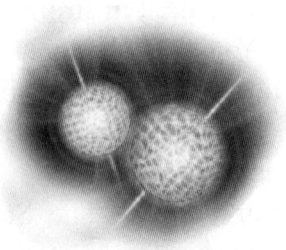

33: Overload

Tark and Zyra sprinted into the common room, straight to Tee.

'We has an idea,' said Tark. 'We needs ta gets ta sum Interface, somewhere close ta the entrance.'

'Why?' asked Tee.

'What are you up to?' added Hope.

'We don't has time ta explain.' Tark's eyes met Tee's. 'I need ya ta trusts me.'

Tee held his gaze for a moment and then spoke. 'Stay here, Hope. Keep an eye on the screen and let me know if anything changes.'

Tee led Tark and Zyra to a side passage in the outer network of caves. It ended in a wall of static.

'The largest we've found,' said Tee.

'Great.' Zyra passed Tark the end of the cable that had a connection point. He plugged it into the back of the IDD. Zyra held out the other end to Tee.

Tee's face went white and he opened his mouth to protest.

'Please,' said Tark. 'Trusts me. Trust *us*!'

Tee hesitated. One look into Zyra's eyes, even though they were not his Zyra's eyes, and he switched off the force-field. Taking the cable from Zyra, he examined it. Tendrils of silver wire hung limply from its end.

'Stand back,' he said, holding up the end of the cable towards the wall of static.

The wire tendrils rose up, reaching out for the Interface. Tee moved the cable closer and wisps of sizzling greyness wound through the air towards the tendrils. When they touched, energy crackled around them and the cable was yanked from Tee's hands, plunging into the depths of the static that was the emptiness between worlds.

The IDD almost jumped from Tark's arms as the raw power of the Interface hit it, filling the syringe in seconds flat. Tark clutched it to his chest as it shuddered.

'I'll stay here,' said Tee, holding up the remote. 'If there's any trouble, I'll switch on the force-field, which will sever the cable and cut the power.'

'Thanks,' Tark said.

'Good luck,' called Tee, as the pair headed out.

The first thing that Tark and Zyra saw as they emerged into the daylight was the light grid which dominated the landscape between the mountains and the Forest. Within it, the Fat Man was on his knees, a waning stream of static surging towards the Static Man. Step by step, the Static Man closed in on the Fat Man.

'Drop the perimeter,' yelled Zyra.

The Fat Man glanced over his shoulder. He saw Tark and Zyra standing at the edge of the light grid holding the IDD between them, and smiled.

'That won't work,' laughed the Static Man. 'It doesn't hold enough power.'

The Fat Man jerked his head to one side and the light grid disappeared.

As Tark flicked the override switch and fired the IDD, the Static Man caught a glimpse of the cable snaking its way from the weapon into the darkness of the Outers' cave. A plethora of faces appeared within the static form of its body, all shouting 'Nooo!'

Tark and Zyra clutched the weapon, desperately trying to hold their position and keep it aimed as lightning blasted from the IDD towards the Static Man.

Hit by the full force of the discharge, the Static Man had time for one guttural howl before it lost its shape.

The energy of the Interface sped along the electric discharge, coursing through the antivirus program, overloading its programming, frying its coding, line by line. Faces appeared within its depths – screaming, contorting faces that disintegrated. Streams of numbers rushed across the surface of the static, each one disappearing – and with each deletion, the program became less and less.

Eyes closed tight against the overpowering glare,

ears ringing with the roaring of the discharge, Tark and Zyra hoped that they were doing the right thing. It seemed like they were frozen in time, their minds playing back their lives. The game, the dangers, the thieving; the World and Suburbia; the Fat Man, the Cracker, Edgar and Vera; love and ice-cream. All messed up and mixed up and blended into one continuous stream that spun relentlessly through their heads.

'Stoppp!' A voice broke into their thoughts.

Zyra cracked open an eye.

It was the Fat Man shouting. 'Stop!'

There was nothing left of the antivirus program. The blazing energy that arced from the IDD was scorching across the ground in random waves, splitting apart the environment, revealing the Interface beyond.

Zyra nudged Tark, who opened his eyes and took in the scene.

'We need ta cuts the power,' he called over the sound of wildly discharging energy as their world ripped apart.

'Can you hold it?' cried Zyra. 'While I get to Tee?'

'I'll try.'

Zyra released the IDD and ran for the cave entrance. The IDD quaked with power as it spewed energy indiscriminately. Tark found himself dragged off his feet. He tried to hold on as long as he could, but it slipped from his grasp and Tark crashed to the stony ground. As it launched up into the air, the syringe shattered and the static burst from it in a short, sharp explosion.

And then all was still and quiet. The haphazard wounds into the Interface healed as if they had never been there.

Tark opened his eyes. Zyra and Tee were running from the cave towards him. He staggered to his feet and found himself in Zyra's embrace.

When they released each other, they saw the Fat Man lying unmoving on the ground. His eyes flickered open when they approached.

'So, it worked?' said Tee.

'Yes,' the Fat Man gasped. His eyes closed and his body disappeared in a shimmer of light.

'The Ultimate Gamer,' said Tark at the same time as Zyra cried, 'Bobby!'

The three of them ran for the common room.

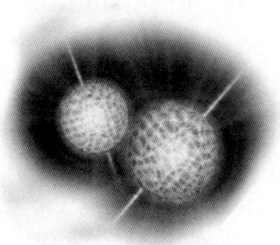

34: Goodbyes

Hope was staring up at the podium when Tark, Zyra and Tee ran in. The Ultimate Gamer wavered unsteadily, his form blackened and charred. The loops of gold were barely moving at all.

'He don't looks too good,' said Tark.

'I think he's dying,' added Hope.

Zyra ran up to the foot of the podium. 'Are you going to be all right?'

The Ultimate Gamer slowly shook his head.

'What about Bobby?' Zyra persisted. 'Is he you? Is he okay?'

'We are each other's avatars.' The Ultimate Gamer's voice was weak and crackly. 'We are two sides of the same coin. He is the desire to play. I am the ability.'

The loops stopped spinning and fell from the podium, dispersing into dust when they hit the ground.

The Ultimate Gamer shuddered and slowly

leaned forward. As the podium crumbled beneath him, he fell.

Bobby hit the ground at Zyra's feet, his clothing singed and smoking.

'Bobby,' she gasped.

'No more games,' he said, lying still. 'No more winning.'

'Oh, Bobby.' Zyra's eyes misted over.

'I wanted to play forever.' A tear welled up in the corner of Bobby's eye, trailed down his cheek and splashed onto the dusty ground. 'Damn the Designers.'

His eyes closed, his breathing ceased and he began to shimmer.

'Wait,' called Hope. 'What about the cheat code? How do we get out of here?'

'I am the key,' Bobby whispered, even though his lips were still.

One by one, solid particles became shining pixels, until their light faded and Bobby's body was no longer there. In its place something began to take form – a small oblong.

As it solidified into plastic, Zyra realised what it was. 'A Designers Paradise key,' she breathed.

Tark and Zyra, and Hope and Tee formed a semicircle around the key, gazing down at it in reverence.

Hope bent down and snatched it up, turning it over in her hands. It was white and blank – no logo, no embedded chip, nothing. 'Now what?'

Tee took the key. He too examined it. 'We find a way to use it.'

'Bobby was scared of whatever is out there,' said Zyra. 'He wanted to stay inside the game.'

'Maybe we need to take this to the Oracle,' said Hope, ignoring Zyra.

'We is Outers,' said Tark. 'It won't interacts with us.'

'Maybe it will only work for a particular person,' suggested Tee. He held it out to Zyra.

Zyra reached out hesitantly with her forefinger and thumb, stopping millimetres short of the key. She took a deep breath, held it, glanced over at Tark, and gently took the key.

Nothing happened.

She released her breath and looked to Tark. He shrugged and took the key. It glowed briefly, and then went dull again.

Tark and Zyra stared at each other.

'Both of you,' said Tee. 'It needs both of you.'

'No way!' complained Hope. 'Why them? It should be me.'

Tee put a gentle hand on his daughter's shoulder. 'It doesn't really matter who gets out, so long as someone does.'

'It matters to me,' said Hope. 'I always thought it would be me . . . us. You and me. Father and daughter – out in the real world.'

'It's better this way,' Tee assured her. 'It feels right that it's Tark and Zyra. It was the original Tark and Zyra who, long ago, were the first Outers. It was me and my Zyra who had a child to fulfil the cheat code. And now it is this Tark and Zyra who will step out of the game.'

Hope's shoulders slumped a little in acceptance.

Tark held out his hand to Zyra. She smiled and took it.

'Zyra!' Hope hesitantly stepped towards her. 'I . . . I never knew my mother.' She hurriedly searched for the right words. 'I'm not saying you're her, because you're not. You're not my mother. But . . . thanks for sticking with me.'

Zyra smiled and faced Tee. He didn't say anything – but his expression spoke of repeated loss and new hope. Zyra mouthed the words 'Old Man' and squeezed Tark's hand.

'Let's go,' she whispered.

'Wait,' said Tark. 'It all started with a kiss.'

Zyra's smile broadened and she leaned in to kiss Tark. As their lips met, she touched the card.

01100101 01111000 01101001 01110100 glowed across the surface of the key.

Everything they had ever known melted away as Tark and Zyra finally, irreversibly, left the game.

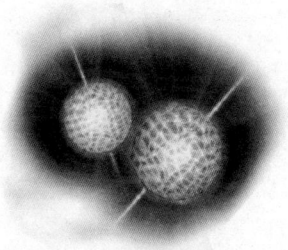

Acknowledgements

My thanks to Ford Street for publishing this book and its predecessor, and for all the great feedback and assistance the staff provided.

As always, my wife, Kerri, who read and commented on my outline and early drafts. This time around she was also instrumental in the shaping of the story, courtesy of a brainstorming session during a long drive out to the country. I am indebted to her in so many ways.

And for inspiration I must acknowledge William Gibson's *Neuromancer* for its dead channel sky; Steven Moffat's *Doctor Who* episode 'The Empty Child' for its terrifying image of WWII gasmasks; *Star Trek* for its communicators; and the terrific YA anthology *Zombies vs Unicorns*, edited by Justine Larbalestier and Holly Black – after reading this anthology I had to have both zombies and unicorns in *Gamers' Challenge*.

More great reading from Ford Street Publishing

50 GOOD REASONS TO READ
TRUST ME!

JUSTIN D'ATH
SALLY ODGERS
ROBERT HOOD
DEBORAH ABELA
LUCY SUSSEX
BILL CONDON
DIANNE BATES
CORAL TULLOCH
HAZEL EDWARDS
ALLAN BAILLIE
KEITH TAYLOR
JENNY BLACKFORD
MICHAEL PRYOR
SEAN MCMULLEN
GEORGE IVANOFF
CAROL JONES
DAVID RISH
JIM SCHEMBRI
SIMON HIGGINS
MEREDITH COSTAIN
KERRY GREENWOOD
RICHARD HARLAND
SOPHIE MASSON

LILI WILKINSON
SALLY RIPPIN
SCOT GARDNER
JENNY MOUNFIELD
KATE FORSYTH
SUE BURSZTYNSKI
GARY CREW
MARC MCBRIDE
ANDY GRIFFITHS
PHILLIP GWYNNE
JANET FINDLAY
LOUISE PROUT
DAVID METZENTHEN
DAVID MILLER
STEVEN HERRICK
MITCH VANE

DOUG MACLEOD
JAMES ROY
SHERRYL CLARK
MICHAEL WAGNER
SOFIE LAGUNA
CATHERINE BATESON
MEME MCDONALD
SHAUN TAN
LEIGH HOBBS
GRANT GITTUS
ISOBELLE CARMODY

Edited by Paul Collins
Introduction by ISOBELLE CARMODY

www.fordstreetpublishing.com   FORD ST

More great reading from Ford Street Publishing

QUENTARIS
QUEST OF THE LOST CITY

The Spell of Undoing
by Paul Collins

Calamity has befallen the city of Quentaris!

Due to a vengeful plot by warlike Tolrush, Quentaris is uprooted – city, cliff-face, harbour and all – and hurled into the uncharted rift-maze. Lost and adrift in this endless labyrinth of parallel universes, encountering both friend and foe, the city faces a daunting task. Somehow, Quentaris must forge a new identity and find its way home.

And nothing is ever as easy as it seems ...

www.fordstreetpublishing.com

FORD ST

More great reading from Ford Street Publishing

BEFORE THE STORM

'... clever plot, feisty characters ... this is a great story'
Kerry White

Fox and BC travel through time from the distant future to 1901. Elite cadets in the Imperial Army, they are young, handsome, well-mannered ... and now, mutineers.

They have journeyed into the past to save the opening ceremony of Australia's first parliament from being bombed. If the cadets fail, thousands will die, sparking a century of total war.

However, to change the destiny of the world, the young warriors will need the help of three ordinary teenagers ...

About the author

Sean McMullen is one of Australia's leading SF and fantasy authors, with fourteen books and sixty stories published, for which he has won over a dozen awards.

His most recent novels are *The Ancient Hero* (2004) and *Voidfarer* (2006). When not writing he is a computer training manager, and when not at a keyboard he is a karate instructor.

www.fordstreetpublishing.com   FORD ST

More great reading from Ford Street Publishing

My Extraordinary Life & Death
Doug MacLeod

What exactly is The Tight Trouser Club?
Where do you buy children at bargain prices?
How do you survive a father who buries you in the garden whenever you misbehave?
And whom do you contact when your wife starts to shrink?

None of these questions are answered in *My Extraordinary Life and Death*, though what do you expect if the author admits that he is dead?

A roller-coaster of madness and surreal comedy awaits the reader brave enough to open this truly remarkable book.

www.fordstreetpublishing.com

More great reading from Ford Street Publishing

In a galaxy of cutthroat companies, shadowy clans and a million agendas, spy agency RIM barely wields enough control to keep order.

Maximus Black is RIM's star cadet. But he has a problem. One of RIM's best agents, Anneke Longshadow, knows there's a mole in the organisation.

And Maximus has a lot to hide …

www.fordstreetpublishing.com   **FORD ST**

More great reading from Ford Street Publishing

They told me I had to write this
by Kim Miller

Clem is a boy in strife. Blamed for the death of his mother, carrying a terrible secret from the past and in trouble with the police, he's now in a school for toxic teenagers. And that rev-head school counsellor wants him to write letters. Through his writing Clem goes deep into the trauma that has defined his life. Then he comes face to face with his mother's death.

In a rush of bush bike-racing, the death of one student and the consequent arrest of another, an unexpected first girlfriend, and some surprising friendships, Clem's story is the celebration of a boy who finds an unforeseen future.

"A compelling story that offers an insight into the life of a troubled teen who ultimately finds freedom."
Terry O'Connell
Australian Director, Real Justice

www.fordstreetpublishing.com

FORD ST